Envious queen

In a small town lived an ugly sick girl with her parents. They loved her and felt sorry for her, brought doctors, but in vain - the girl continued to get sick and was so thin that it seemed that the wind would blow, lift her up and take her away - she was so thin. Around the house she was only allowed to brush off the dust. She could not even lift a broom - she was so weak, although she ate well. She often caught a cold, coughed.

And then one day her father was at work, and her mother was weeding the beds in the garden. The girl was sitting on the porch, playing with dolls. An unexpectedly unknown woman ran up to her, pretty, tired and all out of breath. Approached her and asked:

- Evil guys are chasing me and want to kill me, but I'm not to blame for anything. Hide me.

They had a hole in the closet under the floor, where they put supplies for the winter, if the hole in the kitchen under the floor was full. So the girl hid the woman there, and even locked the door. And she sits on the porch and plays with dolls. She poured water into a cup and watered the doll, saying:

- Drink Manyasha, beauty, or you will get sick like me.

Disheveled men run up to her, four of them, and ask menacingly:

- Well, tell us where a young woman in a flowery dress and a polka dot scarf ran.

- Uncles, I didn't see anyone. Not even a bird flew by. Who are you looking for? Tired, probably. And let me treat you to tea, although Manyasha has already drunk everything from me.

The peasants got even more angry, pushed the girl and searched the house, but finding nothing, they did not take anything. They looked under the floors in the cellar in the kitchen, but they did not find the woman. Angry and dissatisfied, they ran to look further.

The girl rubbed her bruised places, walked around the house, making sure that the pursuers had left, opened the door in the closet and let the woman out of the darkness, and then her mother came from the garden. And heard the story:

- The pursuers are bad men. They killed a girl, my neighbor, and I myself saw everything and wanted to tell the authorities. So they chased me, but I've been running fast since childhood, so no one could ever catch up with me. So I came running to you. It was good that the hiding place was cunning and the killers did not find me.

The woman looked at the girl, stroked her head and said:

- I bless you for your kindness and help. I'm not a simple aunt, but a healer. I will heal you. From this day on, you will be beautiful, healthy, and when you grow up, you will marry a prince. And now I will go to the forest - there in a house in the swamps and I will live until these murderers are caught. Behind the swamp, behind the forest, my cousin lives, I can take refuge with her. For now, I can't show myself to people, because there are envious people. They will tell the killers about me, - she tied up the scarf. - It's already evening. I'll go. Thank you for your help, sorry.

Then the girl's father came, they told him what had happened. Here they all together persuaded the woman to stay overnight:

- Where are you going to go at night? Dangerously. In the morning you will start your journey.

The fugitive agreed, and early in the morning, just before dawn, the three of them went to the forest to see her off. They took a saw, an ax, a rope and left on a horse, instructing their daughter to stay at home and not go out anywhere, not let anyone in.

- Where will I go? I don't even have girlfriends," the girl said sadly.

So the parents went to the forest for a whole week, and the woman lived there in a hut, while they helped her repair a small hunting lodge so that she hid there, and then they rarely visited her. They just came to report that the bandits had finally been caught and she was now free to return home.

A week later, the woman returned, and not empty-handed, but with a pot of fragrant broth. And she gave a pot, instructing the girl to drink three times a day after meals with a prayer. And she said a prayer:

How strong are the grasses in the forest,

How beautifully they bloom

And so you flourish

Gain strength day by day

Never get sick again.

And at that moment the sun itself smiled out the window. Parents looked at each other: how did the sun suddenly appear on this gloomy day?

- You really are special, - said the father.

The girl has been getting better since then. She was no longer sick, she went to school, her cheeks became pale pink from eternally pale, her lips became plump bows. And she became pretty in the face, and over time she completely became a beauty, that there was no one more beautiful in the area. Parents even began to fear for her. Previously, they were worried that she was ill, but now that someone might come to steal their beloved, because their hut was on the edge of the forest, all sorts of wanderers walked by. Out of fear, they even brought in a large, vicious dog.

The girl grew up and turned into such a kind beauty, a needlewoman, like a fairy. Everything went well with her, she knew how to embroider, sew, and such things that the great masters did not even have such products.

And in this state there lived a king and a queen, a beauty, but she only did that she showed off and was jealous of her husband for everyone, did not allow him to look at others: she wanted her to be the only superstar of his eyes. She wanted to please everyone, so that everyone admired her beauty. As soon as she gets a little sick, she immediately gets into bed and dozens of doctors fuss, revolve around her. In any free time, she only did what she demanded special attention to herself and admired herself in the mirror, looking for if there were any girls more beautiful than her in the kingdom. Only what seemed pretty to her, she was immediately expelled from the state. Therefore, she kept the most unpretentious inconspicuous servants with her.

Their son grew up - soon it was time for him to marry. And the mother herself began to look for brides for him, but she looked for such ugly princesses, and wherever she found them - the king himself was surprised, but was silent. He loved her for her beauty, and she still wasn't evil. Especially all his life, the mother did not deal with her son, he was brought up by nannies.

The subjects once brought to the queen portraits of all overseas princesses, various princely daughters. The queen sat down at the table and began to carefully examine them: one has too big, beautiful eyes, the other has a charming smile. The third camp is like a swan, and this one is just a feast for the eyes. The Queen's head is spinning.

- Yes, what is it? Why are they all so beautiful? Everyone is trying to outshine me. It won't work," she shook her head.

And at this time the prince came to visit his mother and, seeing a bunch of portraits, boiled:

- Mommy, what is it with you?

And she convulsively began to rake up all the portraits in one heap:

- Yes it is, nothing, my future retinue.

And the young prince is not a fool, he realized that his mother was already looking for a bride. He bowed and went out, but remained under the door. And he hears: the queen shook off all the portraits and began to trample them angrily, saying, gritting her teeth:

- I will not let it! Even their feet will not be in my house! I will crush all these beauties! I'm sweeter and prettier than everyone else, and I'll find the worst one for my son!

The prince heard this and even the blood rushed to his head from his mother's speeches:

- Wow, mommy made it up? Absolutely, looking at herself in the mirror, she lost her mind! I won't marry a terrible one, I myself will find who I want, - he got angry and jumped out of the palace.

He saddled his horse and galloped wherever his eyes looked, and then, driving his horse into the soap, when the horse was already plaintively neighing, rearing up, only then the prince stopped and was surprised at his recklessness. He stroked the wet mane of the horse, apologizing:

- Ah, my poor friend, forgive my friend, I drove you, - he dismounted, looked around. - Where am I? - surprised.

In front of him was a dark, dense forest, and at the very edge of it stood a low house. The guy knocked and, not hearing an answer, went into the house to ask for a drink and a horse to drink. And there, in the upper room, sat a girl of indescribable beauty. She sits and embroiders with beads. The prince, as he entered, was stunned, he even forgot that he wanted to get drunk. And the girl got scared, jumped up, dropped her sewing. The guy jumped to pick it up, she recoiled.

- I'm sorry ... I'm a traveler ... I don't know ... it's how I got here ... I apologize again. I didn't want to scare you, and in no way offend you... I didn't understand how I ended up here. I galloped, galloped and got lost ... I just wanted to ask for water for myself and my horse ... - and with these words he picked up the needlework and handed it to the girl. She calmed down a little and put the beads on the table.

- What is your name? Where will you be from? - she asked softly.

- I'm Prince Arthur.

- Oh, - she threw up her hands. -Your Highness, - and she wanted to bow to him, but he grabbed her by the shoulders and did not let her fall at his feet.

The girl blushed all over:

- Oh, how embarrassing. I have nothing worthy to treat you with. There is only our peasant.

- I don't mind, - the prince was delighted and sat down at the table.

The girl shyly lowered her gaze.

- There are no gourmet dishes, but I can treat you to milk with blueberry pie. I baked myself.

The prince nodded happily. He liked the girl so much that he was ready to eat anything from her hands.

Having taken her treats, he licked his lips:

- Ah, I have never tasted anything better in my life! - Such a pleasure!

The hostess blushed again and from under her brow looked embarrassedly at the guest, smiling at him. The prince got up, brushed off his camisole and asked where the horse could get water to drink, if they had a well here. And then only he noticed beautiful multi-colored bouquets on the walls, all made of beads, as if alive. And different animals. All these embroidered canvases made the hut brighter and more beautiful. They were so beautiful that the prince could not resist and came close to them, began to look at them, touch them with his hand, stroke them, marveling at the craftsmanship, love and grace with which they were made.

- And how do you like it?

- Of course, it's amazing! I don't even have words! I can't even believe it was made by human hands. Is it embroidered by you?

- Yes, I did them. I really like to embroider. And my mother sells them at the market.

The guy lowered his hands, went to the buckets and asked:

- Take me to the well.

The girl retorted:

- Oh, what are you? How can you yourself? I will bring water to the horse, - and I wanted to take away the bucket from him.

- What are you? You are doing such delicate work, how can you lift such a heavy bucket? Leave it to the man.

- No, that's not right. And I have a papa ... that's how it is with us.

- It won't be like that from now on. I will send my servant to help you. It is not good for such a beautiful girl to spoil her white hands.

- What are you, the right is not worth it, - the girl still tried to resist, although her rosy cheeks betrayed the pleasure that she was very pleased with such attention and care for her. - Daddy will misunderstand. And the neighbors will judge...

- Nothing, I will come again and ask permission from your parents, if you will let me.

- Well, you are always welcome here, you are welcome, - and her face lit up with a wide smile, from which the prince spread warmth over his chest.

He, satisfied, began to water the horse, forgetting about everything in the world, and about his incident with his mother, and about their misunderstanding - a disagreement in the upcoming marriage. And the girl rushed headlong to her secret box, in which she put a bag for coins, specially embroidered by her with mother-of-pearl-pink beads for her future chosen one.

The prince came to say goodbye, and she, looking down, handed him her modest gift:

- Accept a gift from me, a bag for coins.

The prince took her hand with the bag and pressed it to his heart:

- Thank you, girl, thank you, beautiful. I really like your gift.

Kissing her hand, he took out gold coins from his pocket and put them in a new bag. Throwing it into the air, he caught it on the fly, listening to the sound of coins, slyly narrowed his eyes:

- It will definitely come in handy for me, - and plugged it into the belt.

The girl explained to him how to get to the nearest village, and from there straight to the palace. Saying goodbye, he jumped on his horse and rode off. She waved her hand at him.

All the way the prince thought about the beautiful girl, remembering with regret that he even forgot to ask her name.

She didn't stop thinking about him either. When her parents came home, she told about the noble guest, and they were delighted with this, immediately remembering the healer's prophecy. What if their daughter really becomes the wife of a prince?

As soon as the prince returned home, he already heard rumors from the servants that the mother was going to organize her son's wedding. The guy hit himself on the sides:

- Eh, mother, mother, your plans will not come true. I will marry the one I want, - and hastened to tell his father about what had happened.

- Papa, I want to tell you something important, - he shouted from the threshold: - Mama wants to marry me against my will!

- Well, son, the time has already come, so she is looking for a bride for you, - the king shrugged.

- Daddy, you don't know, she's looking for the most terrible bride for me, so that her beauty won't be overshadowed. And I already found a girl for my heart. And I think that I would marry her. She is so sweet, as her figure is thin and stately, and her sonorous voice rings like a stream. And how beautifully it embroiders with beads, you cannot even imagine. And she bakes pies that even our chef could not come up with.

The king was surprised:

- What is it, son? When did you have time to eat pies? Where were you and where did you find her? Did you go to her house?

- Father," the prince hurried to explain, - you misunderstood everything. I'll tell you everything now.

And he began to tell how he was offended by his mother and galloped aimlessly, got lost and came across a hut. How he came in to ask for water, and left his heart there.

- Daddy, it seems I can't live without her, - and he handed his father a gift. The king looked, turned it over in his hands, shaking his head in surprise:

- What fine work. She is indeed a craftswoman.

As soon as the king found out about the beautiful girl, the needlewoman, he did not believe that she was disinterested and he decided, secretly from his son, to check if she was really a good girl. He loaded a whole wagon of precious goods, sable furs, spoiled outfits, silver and gold, and went with his servants to see her, dressed as merchants. He found a handsome serf to pass him off as a noble lord, dressed him up and arrived at the house where the needlewoman lived.

Hearing noise in the street, the girl's parents ran out into the yard. And there, on a huge, full of all sorts of good cart, covered with a carpet, sits a burly merchant and next to him is a handsome, prominent guy. There are two more on horseback in the back.

- Peace to your home. We are visiting merchants. We heard, you have a marriageable bride, so we came to woo her. And we already have a handsome fellow, but not empty-handed, - the king pointed to his fellow traveler and to the cargo.

The husband and wife were surprised and invited to enter the house. They sat down on benches covered with linen bedspreads. They poured them kvass from the road, pulled it out of the cellar and put pork jelly with garlic, pickled cucumbers, and crispy mushrooms on the table, cut the bread into slices. They wanted to add more treats, but the king stopped them:

 - Enough for the meal already, the food is already enough. Now I'll treat you too, - he waved his hand and the servants brought in baskets full of smoked sturgeon, dried venison, honey, sweets and spices.

  The woman threw up her hands. With a bow and a smile, she and her husband accepted the merchant's gifts. The guests looked around and the king asked:

 - And where, in fact, is your beauty? Why doesn't she welcome guests?

  The owner hastened to answer:

 - She went to the pasture to milk the goat. Now she will bring fresh milk.

 - Oh, she milks your goat too?

 - Of course, - said Mother proudly. - She is a master of all trades. From morning till night she works around the house, but she embroiders such canvases, and I sell them, - she pointed to the walls.

- Oh, what a beauty! - the king sincerely admired, and thought: the son, it seems, knowingly fell in love with her. If she is also as beautiful as the craftswoman, then the son was not mistaken. But we will check this.

And then the girl appeared at the door with a jug of milk in her hands. The guy who pretended to be the groom stood up. The king gestured for him to sit down. The girl stood on the threshold as if rooted to the spot. And her parents rushed to explain to her that the matchmakers had arrived. Silently she put the pot on the table and does not say a word. And the king himself stood up and bowed slightly:

- And here is our handsome groom, nice to meet you. You are a perfect match. Both are beautiful and stately.

The girl immediately blushed with embarrassment, covering her face with a handkerchief. She wanted to say something, but the king interrupted her:

- We are not interested in the dowry, we have enough of our own good. Hey, assistants, - he shouted to the servants, - bring in here.

And after a couple of minutes, chests with jewels, rolls of silk, gold brocade, caskets with pearls and sapphires were brought into the upper room and placed on the floor. The astonished parents, with their mouths open, their eyes wide, did not know what to say. And the king watched the girl all this time, but did not see greed and special delight in her eyes. He thought about it and decided to ask her:

- Aren't you happy about all this, girl? Or did they bring you little, or do you not want to get married?

- I want to get married, - the girl murmured softly, "but there is already someone who is dearer to me than anyone else in the world.

The king was delighted with such speeches and continued to test the girl:

- And who is this lucky man who is better than my nephew?

And as soon as she opened her mouth to say that this was a prince, when her parents stood up and interrupted her so that she would not blurt out and make the people laugh. The mother tugged at her daughter's sleeve and answered herself, fearing that they would be laughed at if they told the truth:

- Yes, we have one hard-working guy here in the village ...

- Hmm, we were late, that means, - the king patted the serf on the shoulder. - Well, then we ask you to excuse us, God help you.

The servants loaded all the precious gifts back into the cart, bowed and left home. All the way the king thought:

- Hmm, it's a pity if she really has someone, and why not. What a worker, smart, beautiful, she will be better than secular ladies. It's a pity to lose such a daughter-in-law, - he twisted his mustache in thought.

Returning to the palace, he went straight to his son's chambers. Caught him looking at a present.

- Here, son. I thought I was here and I want to ask you.

- Yes, father, ask.

- You've fallen in love and intend to marry, but what about the girl? What other feeling did you take for her love? Or maybe she already has someone else?

The prince jumped up in fright:

- Can not be! Is that possible?! Daddy, we must urgently go there and ask her.

 - So it is so, but what will your mother say? She probably won't be happy.

 - But we won't tell her, - it dawned on the prince.

- Well, first we will find out if the girl loves you, and then I myself will settle with my wife.

 And the next day, waking up before everyone else in the palace, they went together to the house of the beauty.

 - I won't go there, I'll stand behind the trees, I'll watch, and you yourself talk to her. She will be ashamed of me, - said the king and dismounted, tying his horse to a branch. - And you, son, go, then you will tell me everything.

So they decided.

The prince knocked on the window. His lover appeared at the knock. She saw the prince and threw up her hands in surprise, was delighted and rushed headlong to open the door.

-      Prince, are you back? - and for joy did not know what to say.

He took her hand and asked:

- From the first time we met, I thought about you all the time. And now I came to ask: will you marry me?

The girl lowered her eyes, flushed with embarrassment and did not answer. He pressed her hands to his chest, his heart pounding with excitement. He pulled her hands away from him.

- Well, why are you silent ... Or do you not like me? Or is there someone else in your heart?

She got scared and shook her head.

- No, no! - she exclaimed, - I have no one.

- Then why don't you answer?

She lowered her eyes again and took a deep breath.

- Well, I'm not equal to you, I'm a commoner.

The prince was hopeful and again happily grabbed her hand:

- What you? You are more valuable to me than any princess. Yes, I can't live without you! - exclaimed in the hearts. - Say yes!

- Yes, - she breathed out, barely audible, and clung to his chest.

He gently hugged her at that moment, the king appeared from behind the trees. The girl saw him, got scared and jumped back:

- Oh, - she held out her hand. - There is a merchant coming. Yesterday he wooed me for his nephew.

The prince stood with his back to the forest, turned around and smiled when he saw his father, and then frowned:

So this is my father? Daddy, I'm asking for an explanation. To what kind of nephew were you going to give my fiancee?

Papa slowly approached, giggling guiltily and shrugging his shoulders:

- He-he, well, you know, son, I should have checked your chosen one. Is she worthy of you, is she not greedy for gold. What if for her clothes and jewelry are more valuable than you?

Here the girl pouted her lips. And the king continued:

- And now I see that you deserve each other.

The couple immediately cheered up and exhaled easily. The prince grabbed the bride's hand, approaching his father, and both knelt down. The son asked his father:

- Bless us, father.

The King touched their foreheads with a satisfied smile and said:

- I bless you, my children, for a long and happy life together.

   Her parents arrived from the market. She kindly greeted them, laid a tablecloth on the table for them all. The king and the prince were delighted and immediately wooed the girl, saying that she would marry him. Parents and daughter agreed to have a wedding in the palace. And the king nevertheless decided to tell his wife that he had decided to marry his son to a village girl. And upon returning to the palace, he went straight to her.

   - How?! - furrowing her brows and pursing her lips, the queen murmured: - Well, I already found a bride for him, it doesn't happen more beautifully, just look. Royal bloodlines. Why do we need a rustic? Here, look, her portrait. Check out what a beauty!

   The king looked and thought:

   - God, it doesn't get any worse. Does my son deserve better? - and said aloud: - Do not worry, my love. This village girl will not be more beautiful than you anyway. You should only see her: neither your grace, nor sophistication. She doesn't even know how to wear royal outfits. Where does she reach for you? That's why I chose the country one, so as not to overshadow you.

   - Yes?! - her face smoothed out, she raised her head high and said with mock pride: - You're right, dear, there is some truth in this.

Her cutesy manner seemed to make her head and shoulders taller. And the king embraced his wife, kissed her on the forehead, that the woman blossomed.

At the imminent wedding, the queen was sitting on the throne, she was surrounded by ladies-in-waiting, preening her, bringing a mirror to check if any curl had fallen. The ceremony was already in full swing, the feast was a mountain, the music was playing. A sea of distinguished guests gathered. The queen did not even look in the direction of her daughter-in-law - she did not care what kind of ugly girl was brought to the palace. She just admired herself in the mirror, saying:

- What a beauty I am, you can't find such a beauty in the whole wide world, - and as if in time with her speeches, she heard the whisper of the crowd: - Oh, what a beauty!

The queen turned up her nose: yes, I am! But then she heard a continuation of the speech:

- What a lovely couple. What a beautiful bride, and you can't say that she's not a princess.

- Bride?! What bride? - the queen raised an eyebrow in surprise and turned towards the newlyweds and, seeing her daughter-in-law, was stunned: an unwritten beauty stood next to her son.

- Who is it? Who dragged her? Changed! Was there a villager there? - and with her eyes she began to look for her husband, expecting an explanation from him. Not finding him nearby, she turned to the maid of honor, deciding that she was mistaken: - And how exquisite she is in a wedding dress. And a diamond necklace suits her. I have never seen such a princess?

Involuntarily admiring her, she forgot. The maid of honor just batted her eyelashes stupidly, not daring to comment on anything. And then the queen started up, as if waking up from a dream:

- So this is that redneck? - If that doesn't happen, I'll think of something! Only I alone will be the most beautiful in this kingdom. I'll take it out, and I'll find another for my son, - she threw the mirror on the floor with anger, jumped up. And convulsively fanning her face, she passed through the crowd, nervously pushing the courtiers aside. - My feet won't be here, - she hissed angrily under her breath, rushing to her chambers.

The bride and groom were so intoxicated with love and did not take their eyes off each other that they did not notice the absence of the queen. Everyone was dancing, lightly circling around the hall. The hall was full of colorful outfits. The king noticed how his wife quickly left the guests, and, apologizing to noble persons, followed her.

- What happened, dear, why did you leave the ceremony? Let's go, everyone is waiting for us.

- I'm not going anywhere, go alone. I got a headache.

- Are you sure you weren't offended by anything? - He gently lifted her chin and slyly looked into her eyes.

- No, really, just a headache from the noise. I'll be back later, don't leave the guests, - she was cunning, pretending to be tired.

 - Well, dear, take care of yourself, rest, - and, kissing his wife on the cheek, he left.

Left alone, the queen began biting her lips as she concocted a plan to get rid of her daughter-in-law.

 - Oh, - how indignant the queen was, she was crying, twitching her upper lip and biting closer: - how can I exterminate my daughter-in-law?

 The girl's parents went home after the feast, and the prince and his wife were so happy and loved each other that they did not part for a minute. Even a short separation caused them pain. But the main affairs of the father pushed love into the background.

One day, the prince and the king went on business to a neighboring state to sign peace agreements. They were gone for a week. The Queen, seizing the moment, rubbed her hands and said smugly, smiling:

 - Now is the right time, I should not miss this chance.

 She called the servants and ordered to secretly steal the daughter-in-law from her chambers at night, so that no one would see and take her to an abandoned castle, which was located far beyond the forest in the swamp. And imprison her there like a prison. Together with the servant girl, she sent a chest of jewelry there, sarcastically remarking that it was not appropriate for a noble lady to look bad there:

- A lady must be a lady even in a swamp. And this lady only belongs there, next to the frogs and mosquitoes.

 She ordered everyone to be silent, otherwise they would lose their lives. Here, from fear for their lives, the servants involved in this were silent.

In the morning the whole palace was raised to its feet: the daughter-in-law was gone! What? How? The guards rushed to the queen and fell at her feet:

- We ask for mercy, empress, you did not order us to be executed. We have not seen who and how kidnapped your daughter-in-law.

- Oh, trouble! What will I say to the poor son? - the queen made a sour face and looked up from the mirror, brushed away an artificial tear from her eyes with a satin handkerchief: - You are not to blame. I have already been informed that this scoundrel ran away at night to her lover and even took jewelry with her.

Soon, the sad news of treason spread throughout the state. The king and his son rushed in and, not seeing the girl, rushed to ask the queen if people were really saying where she had gone. And she answers:

- Yes, she had already married another during this time, she could not wait. Apparently she did not love you, your redneck, my beloved son.

The son did not believe his mother, but did not say anything to her. He yearned for his wife day and night, grew thin - did not eat anything. He sits at the table, they bring him food, and the food gets stuck in his throat - only his beloved wife was before his eyes. He could not believe that such sincere love was a game, that his beloved had betrayed him. She was so humble, with a pure heart. There was no way she could do this to him.

Something else, something bad happened to her. We need to go look for her.

And then the mother decided to console her son, brought him a bride, a princess, but so terrible, crooked, pockmarked, demolished like potatoes, with little eyes. She smiled at the prince, and her teeth sticking out in different directions were also fastened with braces. The prince was frightened, grabbed his hat and cloak on the move and ran headlong away. He ran away from the palace, saddling a horse, and rode wherever his eyes looked.

How long, how short, did our prince ride and his horse came across the house of that sorceress woman who cured his wife in childhood. The horse stopped, neighed, shaking its head. The guy jumped to the ground, dusted himself off. Just as he was about to knock, the door was opened and an elderly woman appeared on the threshold:

-Hello king's son, where are you going?- What did you come with? looked him over carefully.

- Yes, that's the trouble happened to me. The wife is missing, beautiful. The world is not dear to me without her, and my mother wants to marry me again to a slanting, pockmarked princess. I can't do this anymore, I'm looking for my beloved wife. But I don't know who to ask.

And the sorceress answered him:

- Come into the house, rest from the road, taste my jelly with milk, otherwise you have completely lost weight. You need to refresh yourself. And there we will decide how to help your grief.

The prince obeyed and entered the room, not even paying attention to how the woman recognized him as a prince. And there on the bench another woman sits and shakes the ball. Different fragrant herbs hang in the corners. Their scent intoxicated him. Even he was drawn to sleep.

-And this is my sister,- she introduced the guest to the woman. - Sit down, don't be shy.

- Oh, prince, we have been waiting for you for a long time. Come in, my dear, you will be a dear guest.

- How do you know me? – only now he was surprised.

Both chuckled and looked at each other.

- Yes, we are such unusual grannies. We, my dear, know a lot of things.

- I need to hurry, look for my wife. I feel like she's in trouble.

- We know, we know. But still, don't rush, first gain strength. Taste our food, sleep, and in the morning we will pick you up and show you the way.

The prince was delighted, cheered up:

- Do you know where she is?

- Of course, we all know.

- Oh, I can't wait, I'm ready to hit the road right now.

-Ah, fidget,- the hostess patted him on the shoulder and seated him on a bench at the table. She poured jelly, cut off a piece of bread, sprinkled it with salt: - Eat and strength will come.

The prince obeyed, began to eat with pleasure, his appetite appeared, and the old women shook their heads, satisfied, and smacked their lips. They greeted him, because they already knew about everything in advance - how could they not help him?

Barely eating, the prince yawned and stretched. They escorted the sorcerer to the bed, put him there, and they themselves read prayers, walk around the room with smoking herbs, they lit a candle. And the prince dreamed that he was standing on a flowering meadow, dragonflies were flying around, butterflies were fluttering. His beloved appears before him, smiles affectionately and says in a low voice:

- Believe me, my love, I did not betray you. I love you like before, even more.

She said this and disappeared. The prince woke up, and the dawn was already dawning outside the window. He lay down again, and before his eyes stands the image of his beloved. And his soul is calm. He realized that in the palace his mother had deceived him, there was no betrayal, as he had thought before.

Everyone ate barley porridge with milk in the morning, the women gave the guest tea with herbs, and he felt cheerfulness in his whole body.

- Here, take the magic grid with you. When you come to the place where your wife is being kept in the swamps, throw it on yourself and become invisible, otherwise you won't be able to overcome thirty warriors armed with an ax and get into the tower of that castle. And then, together under the net, go out unnoticed and come back to us here, - the healer handed him a light net, and her sister handed him a map of the forest:

- From my late husband, a forester left. This is where you'll need it.

He did just that. He thanked them, bowed and galloped towards the swamps.

He rides through the forest, and the trees are getting thicker and thicker, the path is getting narrower and narrower. He sees a large stone standing in the middle of the path and the paths branched out. He looked at the map, but it was not indicated there. He scratched his head, and turned right, towards the swamps, as he reasoned that the frogs croak strongly on that side and it is also clear on the map where the swamps are drawn on the right side. So he let it go there, already feeling in his heart that he would soon meet his beloved. And the prince was not mistaken.

A putrid smell was already in the nose, the quagmire roared ahead, uttering an ominous groan. As soon as he drove closer, he heard a bewitching female voice:

- Boy, why are you so sad? Come to me, you see, I'm bored here alone.

The prince turned around and saw a beautiful girl. She sat waist-deep in the swamp and only slightly splashed the muddy water with her cassock with her hands.

- What do you doubt, prince?- Kikimora winked. - I've been waiting for you.

- Hmm, strange, - the prince thought:- people told me that kikimoras are terrible, these swamp residents are dangerous, but she seems beautiful.

He dismounted and tied his horse. He came closer to find out who she was.

- Do you swim here?- nodded inquiringly.

Kikimora laughed.

- Come on and swim with me.

The prince approached, looked at her beauty, but recoiled: instead of hair, brown algae moved on her

head. The bright green eyes of the swamp beauty beckoned him to her.

-Yes, go away,- he waved. - Of course, you are beautiful, no doubt, but in my heart I have another.

- Oh, I understand, I loved the foolish forest owner Leshy, but he went to the witch Baba Yaga.

The prince only widened his eyes in surprise.

- Okay, I'll help your grief. Over there, you see, behind those tall trees, the tower sticks out?

He stood up on tiptoe, screwed up his eyes, and through the thick haze of fog he could make out the outlines of the cone of the roof.

  - Is that the peak over there?- he pointed with his hand.

  Kikimora nodded and plunged into the bog with a splash and noise, leaving large bubbles behind her, and only the algae from her head still stuck out on the surface of the bog.

   The prince found a strong stick and walked cautiously forward, feeling his way. The frogs croaked uncontrollably, straining and calling to each other:

  -Here he is, he's unskillful, -he's staggering around, he'll dive in and drown.

Having got out of the swamp, he stepped on solid ground, almost burying his nose in the walls of the old castle. Sneaking unnoticed along the wall to the gate, crouched in the reeds, hearing the laughter of the guards. Tipsy, four men in helmets sat on empty barrels and played dominoes.

   The prince threw a net over his head and became invisible. Stepping slowly, he crept past them and slipped inside. He passed through the whole courtyard, along which other guards walked, sheep bleated in the barn and horses neighed. The prince almost stepped on a duck looking for a worm in the ground.

He went up the spiral staircase and opened the door to the room where his beauty was languishing. She sat hunched over the embroidery by the window. A white mouse ran nearby and, squeaking with joy, collected spilled beads. At the feet of the girl stood a chest with the jewels that she allegedly stole.

The prince stood and could not look away, full of tenderness. His wife did not notice. Only then did he remember that he was invisible and tore off the net. The girl screamed in surprise and almost fainted. The prince caught her in time and pressed her to his chest. When they were close, they hugged and she burst into tears with burning tears, and the tears began to fall and turn into beads. By the wall lay a pile of carpets embroidered with beads, and such beautiful patterns - there was nothing there: different flowers and birds, animals, and even a portrait of her beloved husband. And the big wooden chest was full of beads. When the recluse cried on Monday, white beads fell from her eyes, on Tuesday - red, on Wednesday green, and so on in different colors. The prince was surprised

- Is it you who cried so much, my dear little wife, because of separation from me? Now everything will be different. You and I will live happily and not a single tear will roll down from your beautiful eyes.

They both covered themselves with a net and quietly left this prison of a gloomy building made of wild gray stone, roughly hewn. And they went far from the gate, and only then they removed the invisible net.

When the recluse screamed when she saw her husband, alarmed guards came running to her cry. They saw that the room was empty and the window was wide open. They rushed to the window to look, and below at that moment a huge toad jumped from a stone into a swamp.

-Oh,- the men thought. - Probably she drowned herself, - and they crossed themselves. They immediately sent a messenger to the queen to inform her that her recluse could not stand it and committed suicide.

The queen, hearing the news, only shrugged her shoulders and took a mirror to look:

- Well, okay, one less concern, - and calmed down on this.

The prince and his young wife came to the healer and thanked her, gave the net.

- My dear girl, how long have we not seen each other! - the hostess hugged the girl. - I hope you recognize me.

-Of course, how could I forget you?- Thanks to you, I recovered and married such a wonderful person.

- You will stay here, and in the meantime I will meet with my father, I will please him that I have found you. And together we will come up with, decide what to do next, -the prince thought.

It was already night, he mounted his horse and arrived at the palace in the dark. He quietly woke up his father so that his mother would not wake up, both left the bedroom to have a normal conversation.

- Father, I found my beloved. She languished in the swamps, in the old castle.

- AAA! -exclaimed the king. -Who put her in there?

- You won't believe it - mom did it.

- That's a scoundrel! - the king was angry. - I need to teach her a lesson! - and he was about to wake her up, but the son stopped:

- No, papa, remember, you yourself deceived her: you said that you would marry me to a terrible country woman, and you yourself brought a refined beauty to the palace. That's how she got mad at us. For her, you are the light in the window, so do not offend her.

-Hmm,- the anger subsided a little. - Then let's do this: live with your wife in our hunting lodge until we build a new palace for you. Anyway, the queen does not go there, I order the servants to keep everything a secret. Let her calm down. I will surround her with love and she will be forgotten. And time will pass and everything will be fine. Let's put it before the fact, then it won't mind.

The prince and his wife occupied an empty castle - the queen's servants never came there, and the local servants were forbidden to tell his mother that they had returned together. And they lived happily ever after. The king ordered to bring there all the beads, all the embroideries and jewelry from the old castle in the swamps. Even the mouse was taken away, which was the only friend of the poor girl in her captivity.

Mommy diligently, in consolation to her son, all this time offered him a new bride, thinking that her daughter-in-law had drowned herself. But the son pretended to twist, as if in such deep sadness that he only kissed his mother's hand in response and said:

 - I'm a widower, I have nothing more to marry. The memory of my wife is painfully dear to me.

 The queen calmed down that no competitor threatened her anymore and she could calmly look at herself in the mirror every day, saying:

 - Oh, how beautiful and incomparable I am in our kingdom!

 The prince lived with his wife in the new palace, and occasionally came to visit his parents. He has already had three lovely children. The king himself often visited them, and told his wife: I'm hunting. And he went to them with expensive gifts.

And, leaving for receptions with her neighbor friends, the queen noticed how everyone kissed their grandchildren with love and pride. Everyone around was bragging:

 -Oh, my handsome grandson, my lovely granddaughter,- and little pretty children, like toys, ran up to them in smart dresses and tailcoats. Gently kissed their grandmothers hands.

 Once, at one of these balls, it dawned on the queen:

- And why is it that everyone has beautiful grandchildren, but I don't have beautiful grandchildren ?! And no one kisses my beautiful hands?

 And then, as luck would have it, the neighboring queen came up and boasted with pompous arrogance:

- My beauty fades, but it blossoms in my beautiful grandchildren. Look how they dance merrily, frolic.

The queen was seized with envy, as much as a shadow crept over her face: - And why am I worse than her? My grandchildren would be even more beautiful, - and then she remembered with horror: - Oh, I always tried to slip a terrible bride on my son. They would have terrible children! - and imagined her grandchildren from a terrible daughter-in-law: slanting eyes, a nose like a potato, teeth sticking out like a fan. And she cried out in horror: - Fu, what terrible grandchildren!

- What? Who's scary?! What did you say about my grandchildren? - turned to her neighbor in bewilderment.

- No, you don't understand me! - the queen barked in response and, waving her fan convulsively, added: - I urgently need to leave.

On the way, she pushed everyone in the hall. She jumped into the carriage and ordered the coachman to rush to her kingdom:

- We urgently need to look for a beautiful bride for our son!

Knocking down the door with her hands, she flew into her chambers:

- Where is my new beautiful daughter-in-law?!

The servants and courtiers even had their eyes popping out of their foreheads in amazement: hadn't she always needed a terrible one? What suddenly changed?

They collected portraits of all the most beautiful of the most beautiful and young girls of marriageable age. But now she didn't like any of them. She threw them on the floor and trampled:

This one isn't slim enough! This dark-haired, that freckled! This one has a hooked nose! Why is this mole in the wrong place?

She scooped it up off the table and threw it on the floor. At that moment the son entered the room and found his mother trampling, tearing and tossing the portraits, shouting:

- Not pretty enough! I do not need such daughters-in-law!

- Mom, do you want to marry me again?

- Yes son. I want grandchildren, and such beautiful ones, so that they outshine the most beautiful grandchildren of my friends. Let everyone envy me, and not I owe them!

The prince only smiled contentedly, pleased that mother had matured to meet her grandchildren. He said nothing and rushed to inform his father. And so they decided to bring secretly his wife and children. They settled in the farthest corner of the palace, where the queen never went. Usually guests from other kingdoms were placed in these guest rooms.

The next morning, the queen went out into the garden for a walk and a breath of fresh air, accompanied by her ladies-in-waiting. And, inhaling the fresh scent of tender archeas, she enjoyed her walk. Suddenly, with a squeal and a squeak, she was knocked down by two mischievous boys playing catch-up. The queen cried out:

- What's going on here?! Who are these tomboys? How did you get here?

The boys stopped:

- Excuse me, please, - bowed slightly and ran on.

- Hmm, brought up, - the face distorted by anger changed to surprised: - Whose beautiful children are these? Why haven't I seen them before? -She glanced around at the ladies-in-waiting, looking for an answer from them. The girls shrugged.

-Oh, ma'am, I'm sorry, we really don't know,- everyone shrugged their shoulders in embarrassment.

The queen thought:

- Maybe the guests from which kingdom came and did not notify me? This needs to be dealt with.

She turned around, wanted to go to find out the reason where the children were from. And she saw her husband. The king also went into the garden. A girl, who looked about seven years old, stood by the fountain and watched with admiration how goldfish swim. The queen exclaimed:

- My dear husband, could you explain to me where all these children in my garden came from?

At this time, the girl turned around at her cry and, seeing the king, screamed and rushed to meet him:

- Grandpa, grandpa! Here is my dear grandfather!

The queen has already sat down:

- Grandpa? Why? What, did you deceive me? Did you cheat on me for another? Do you have other children? Who is this shameless woman who took you from me? You've been together for so long behind my back that you even have grandchildren already?! - she collapsed from indignation and began to hysterically beat the ground with her hands: - How unfortunate I am!

The ladies-in-waiting tried unsuccessfully to console her. The king, taking his granddaughter by the hand, hurried to his wife:

Don't kill yourself, my love!

Don't you dare call me my love! squealed the woman, kicking away from her husband.

Let me explain everything to you...

- I hate you! I don't need your explanation! Get out with your grandchildren!

- Grandpa, who is this? Why is she angry and crying?

The king began to calm the frightened child:

- Don't worry, baby, everything's fine.

The girl was frightened by the mad woman on the lawn, who sobbed inconsolably and twisted like a snake in hysterical convulsions, and also began to cry.

And at that moment, her parents appeared from the palace. The prince was leading his beautiful wife by the hand, who had only grown prettier with age and motherhood. The girl pushed her grandfather away and ran to her parents:

- Mother Mother!

The queen stopped crying, obsessed with curiosity to whom the child belonged, and opened her mouth in surprise, seeing a ghost come to life in front of her:

- How are you alive? Have you drowned? - forced the maids of honor to raise themselves.

-Alive, as you can see,- she came closer, reassuring her daughter. She bent down to the girl and said: - Don't cry, dear, it's your grandmother.

- Grandmother? - the child was surprised. Why have I never seen her before?

-I'll tell you about it later, my daughter. Now come and kiss your grandmother's hand.

The queen was stupefied with unexpected joy and hugged her granddaughter:

-You are the most beautiful granddaughter in the world. You are my flower.

Smiling with happiness, the king added:

- Look, she is as beautiful as you, she looks like you.

Tears flowed from the queen's eyes.

- Oh, how wrong I was.

And at that moment the boys ran up. They looked with surprise at the adults standing in the garden. The prince introduced his mother to them:

- Look, children, this is your grandmother. Please love and respect.

- Grandmother! - the brothers were delighted and rushed to hug her.

An order was immediately given to convene all the guests from all neighboring states. The next day they organized a magnificent celebration. All the nobility gathered, and it was the queen's turn to introduce her grandchildren to everyone. All the friends were just surprised:

- How so? Why did you hide them from us for so many years?

- And so that no one jinxes them, - she proudly looked around those present and looked admiringly at her grandchildren. She frantically waved her fan, trying to hide her happiness. This time no one left the room.

The King was the happiest man in the world. Finally, his family is fully reunited. He remembered what his wife was a week ago and was horrified. He came to her then, and she stroked her face and said:

- What a beauty you are, only with age you already need to insert Botox, otherwise I will be late and my beautiful face will be covered with wrinkles.

-Yes, you will always be young and beautiful, my love,- he then stroked her silky hair.

She just raised an eyebrow coquettishly:

- Oh, dear, you tell me a lot of good things. From your words, my beauty will not wither, will not wither, like a flower in autumn.

The king kissed his wife on the cheek and left.

Quite a bit of time passed and the queen stopped noticing that she was getting old. She did not notice this, because her grandchildren were already running around the palace and in the garden, laughing loudly, calling her grandmother, affectionately hugging, and from this the whole yard was filled with cheerful children's laughter. How did she not know this before?

And now, two boys and a girl were again playing briskly in the garden in catch-up, colliding with their grandmother, they spread their hands, apologizing, but the queen did not get angry and did not order to punish the children, as for the first time. Laugh at their antics. Then the king appeared and grinned, appreciating such changes in his wife. He took his granddaughter in his arms and kissed her, and the boys hugged their grandfather with the words "our beloved grandfather".

- Look, dear wife, at your sweet grandchildren. Here the eldest grandson looks like me, the second one looks like his father, and the third beauty - just a feast for the eyes - looks like you.

At these words, the queen softened even more and kissed the child on the forehead, shedding tears:

- Oh, how bad I used to be, I didn't know and didn't understand much. I just took care of myself and envied all the other queens that they already had grandchildren, only they were ugly, but still grandchildren. Here is some happiness. My grandchildren are the most beautiful. Why did you keep silent about this for many years?

- Yes, because you resisted the happiness of your son, lived in anger and envy. But I am glad that my beloved has seen the light and we are all happy now.

She wanted to call the prince and her daughter-in-law, making a sad face, but the king led her to that half of the palace, where she had not even looked before and where the most dear and beloved people had recently begun to live.

There, soft carpets were spread on the floor, beaded carpets hung on the walls, and dresses flaunted

in the closet, which even famous couturiers did not make. And hats - the famous Coco Chanel could not make such hats. The Queen gasped, spreading her arms.

-This is all your daughter-in-law's work,- said the king. - Be proud of her.

Then the son and his wife came in, so beautiful and happy that they can't be told in a fairy tale or described with a pen. They bowed to their parents and the queen shed tears of joy, for the first time she asked for forgiveness from her daughter-in-law. And she had already forgiven her. And they lived happily and in contentment with a large friendly family.

The queen ordered to hang canvases embroidered with beads of her daughter-in-law throughout the palace. And all the guests, courtiers and servants walked and admired them.

Seasonal Snow Maiden

In one kingdom-state, near a wild dense forest, there was a village, and a husband and wife and daughter, kind, clever and beautiful, lived in it. Everything would have been fine, but the wife fell ill early and died. And a neighbor, also a widow with a child, went to visit them. And then a little more time passed and the widower decided to marry this widow: together it is easier to endure grief and hardship. She happily agreed and settled with her daughter, who was the same age as his daughter. And the new wife promised the peasant that she would love her stepdaughter as her own daughter and would educate both of them fairly. The man was delighted, anticipating that he would now live happily and carefree, as with his first wife, and everyone would be happy, because there would be order in the house, ready-made food was always on the table when he came home from work tired and hungry, and he worked as a groom in the stable of a rich man. He told his daughter:

- Listen to her and respect. She will be your mother now.

The girl obediently agreed: she loved the priest very much and never contradicted him.

But the wench turned out to be cunning: at first she was already kind, sympathetic, pretending to be what he imagined her, the mistress, to be. At first, a simple woman like that went to him, pretended to be caring, helped to run the house, promised to love his daughter and take care of everyone. Now she only tried on clothes and ate sweetly. Both with their daughter went in silk dresses - where did they get the money for them - they showed off everywhere: in the market, and on the street in front of their neighbors, and to the city fair they went for candy and gingerbread, and the stepdaughter didn't even have a normal dress, she wore old clothes , forever dirty, in patches. All her hands became calloused and scratched. The old bast shoes were worn out, the felt boots were worn out - in the summer the girl generally spanked barefoot. The stepmother said:

- There is not enough money, your dad earns with difficulty. You both need to put aside for your dowry. So be patient, it's hot in summer, why do you need shoes?

And sometimes she became dissatisfied with the work of her stepdaughter, or for no reason will attack her with a fierce beast:

- What a slob, lazy dirty! - and she will also complain to her husband: - your daughter is completely lazy and has lost her conscience, she does not obey me at all and does not fulfill orders - who will marry her like that? - and he looks sadly at his daughter, but she does not contradict, does not justify herself, only lowers her wet eyes and is silent.

Nor did he dare to argue with his wife, and was even a little afraid of her. Of course, he guessed that the stepmother was slandering the girl, but he could not contradict her.

One day he came home early and found his daughter in tears. She sat in the corner behind the stove and quietly wept furtively, complaining to her mother why she had left her. He sat down next to her and stroked her head. She lifted her eyes, red with tears. The man took his daughter by the hand, stroked her palm, and the hand was covered in calluses. He then understood who was working around the house, and who was just resting and moaning that she was tired. Yes, there is nothing to do. Resigned. If he gets divorced, the whole village will condemn him. Looks like his share.

  - Don't cry, baby. Be patient a little, everything will work out, God willing.

  The girl nodded and wiped away her tears.

The father's daughter, she was even smeared all over with soot and in tattered rags, was more beautiful and sweeter than her stepmother's daughter in expensive silks, rouged, with eyebrows, charcoal lined, scarlet cheeks, smeared with beets. There used to be such a beauty sitting at the window, peeling seeds, but waiting for rich suitors, dreaming of a luxurious life. And the neighbor guys laugh at her and look at her grubby half-sister.

  Time goes fast. So the girls have grown up, the time has come for the grooms to come to woo. They will lay pies and donuts on the table, they will pour raspberry liqueur, but the grooms don't even look at their stepmother's daughter. All eyes are on her stepdaughter:

  - Here is my daughter, a ripe berry, what a beauty she was born, clever, craftswoman, - the woman will begin to praise her daughter, but they interrupt her: - But we like the other one. The one that brings food to the table.

  And no matter how many grooms and matchmakers came, no one was interested in the stepmother's daughter. Everyone only needed a mess.

The woman could not stand it, she ran out of bile. She thought, she thought what to do with her and thought up. She decided to get rid of her stepdaughter, otherwise her daughter would remain in girls.

And then one winter, in the most severe frost in December, the peasant told his people that he would go to the city to the market: the owner slaughtered a lame horse and therefore he would go to sell meat.

-I won't be home for two or three days. You can manage it yourself, and I will bring you gifts from the city. And I won't be around for that long until the meat is sold out.

He said goodbye and left, and his stepmother took advantage of his absence. She became more evil than before. Tired of her freeloader and she decided to lime it. Especially the most suitable case fell out: while the husband is not at home.

She went up to her step-daughter and screamed when she was sweeping the floor in the kitchen:

- Get ready, but hurry up! Time does not wait, we will go for brushwood.

- Mother, I brought it on a sleigh yesterday. Enough for us for two days or even three.

- Shut up, you bastard. Let's go together. Soon the roads will be covered with snow, and you will not pass into the forest. Do you want to freeze or freeze us to death? How are we going to heat the oven? Father will return, what will he say?

The one what to do, you can argue with such a woman.

They put a rope on the sleigh, but a bigger, thicker one, and the stepmother mutters:

- I'll show you how to work.

The girl was not used to arguing with her elders and obeyed.

She threw on her old fur coat, tied up with an old mother's downy scarf, put on darned felt boots and followed her stepmother. They got into the sleigh and drove off.

   They arrived in the forest, but drove far. All roads are covered with snow and the horse does not go further. The stepmother screamed:

   - Why are you sitting, lounging like a mistress? We've already arrived. Get down, let's start collecting firewood, - and the first one, like a young one, jumped off the sleigh.

The two of them collected a lot of brushwood, heaped a full sleigh. And then suddenly the stepmother took the rope, grabbed the stepdaughter by the hair, dragged her to the pine tree. She was a heavy and strong woman - she could knock any man off her feet, and what is there to cope with a fragile girl. That's out of the question. She quickly tied her stepdaughter up and tied her to a tree. The girl didn't even resist. Before that, she was sad to live that a fierce death in the forest seemed sweeter than a bitter life with such a vicious hater.

   The woman herself sat on the sleigh, took the reins and laughed so loudly that snow fell from the bushes and fir trees from the branches. She turned the shafts and drove to the village, rejoicing that she had got rid of her stepdaughter. And she smiled all the way under her breath:

- And if she doesn't freeze here, let the wolves tear her to pieces, they also want to eat.

   She turned her horse around, barked at it, and rode away. The girl did not cry, but thought, looking around:

   - What a beauty here, that even dying is not scary. As snow glitters in the sun, the forest is wrapped in snow, like a gentle veil. How beautiful it is here. It's better to die here than from a stepmother's whip.

The birds chirped loudly in the thin frosty air, so that their echo carried throughout the forest. The squirrels jumped, playfully so that the ice branches cracked. She listened: beside her crackled, falling, broken branches. The frost intensified and it became even colder for her. But such joy seized her that the girl, not only to cry, smiled with happiness, looking around all this winter beauty.

And suddenly, out of nowhere, Uncle Frost himself appeared in front of her, with a staff, and an ice ball at the end of the staff. Strong, broad-shouldered, with a snow-covered beard to the chest. His blue eyes looked merrily at the girl with a cunning squint, and his lips broke into a smile, and he himself was covered with frost. She wanted to salute him, but the rope did not give.

- What, beautiful girl, are you doing here alone at such a time? he boomed in a resonant bass.

She didn't even complain.

- Yes, grandfather, I admire all this unearthly beauty!

Her answer so struck Frost that he immediately banged his staff on the ground and the ropes from it fell to the snow. She stood up and bowed low to him.

- Thank you, Father Frost.

- And I know you, you often come here for brushwood and the blizzard told me about you.

- But I see you for the first time.

- No one sees me at all. This is the first time I showed up to you. I know how you live. You are kind and hardworking. You won't go back, and where are you going now? Your stepmother will definitely not leave you alive. And I take you to my assistant. My daughter is still small, and you will help me instead of her, we will manage together with you in the forest, and walk among the trees and see if everything is in order here. And then I'll tell you how to do it. All of this gradually then learn. And now let's go to my wife, the Snow Queen. You will become our seasonal Snow Maiden. Just know that there is one condition and you must fulfill it.

- Father Frost, I agree to everything, I will be your obedient assistant.

He stroked her head with his huge hand in a white fur mitten:

- You are my clever one, in winter you will become a Snow Maiden, and in the spring, after all the snow has melted, you will again turn into a simple girl, as now, but only you should not fall in love with anyone. And if you fall in love as a Snow Maiden, then you will melt, and even I will not be able to help you.

He put the girl on a beautiful ice sleigh and three deer with beautiful spreading horns quickly drove them to his ice palace. Mother and daughter warmly greeted Frost with the girl.

- And here is my new assistant, meet her, take her as your own, - and Uncle Frost hit his staff, then touched the guest with it, and she immediately turned into a Snow Maiden. She was wearing a beautiful robe, embroidered on blue satin with silver and mother-of-pearl pearls, and on her head was the same blue cap with a white fur rim, adorned with a silver crown with a scattering of diamonds.

It seemed to her that she became lighter in weight and taller. And she had another life. When she used to look at the shiny snow, she wanted the same wedding dress, so that it shone like a fairy, but now she had such a dream dress, but even more beautiful, and the cap on her head was also all shiny, and the caftan was embroidered with precious stones and shimmered so in the sun and in the moonlight that ordinary people would not have looked - their eyes would have been blinded by bright colors.

Every day she now walked through the forest and, at the behest of Uncle Frost, watched whether the snow covered the ground everywhere, whether the blizzard fell asleep well in the spruce and pine trees, whether the bears' dens were wrapped in snow so that they would not freeze. The Snow Maiden handed out nuts to the squirrels, threw carrots to the bunnies, grains to the birds, and she herself ate well. All the animals and birds were grateful to her, and the Snow Queen and Uncle Frost did not like her soul, they loved her like a daughter. She and their daughter became friends and at times walked through the woods together. Titmouses, bullfinches and sparrows fluttered over their heads. Sparrows chirped as they jumped near the pines and firs, collecting seeds. Everything in this life seemed to the Snow Maiden fabulous and beautiful. Sometimes Uncle Frost took her for a ride and added frost with her, treating the staff like a magic wand: knocking it on the ground, putting frost on bushes and trees.

-It is necessary,- he said, -to add frost.

They added to the spruce, and after that she became completely white like a bride before the wedding. The river was covered with ice and covered with snow.

Meanwhile, her own father returned from the market, satisfied that he had sold all his goods, bought gifts, but did not find his daughter at home. The wife wiped her eyes with a handkerchief and pretended to be grieving no less than he:

  - Our daughter went to the forest with a sleigh for firewood and did not return, but our filly came alone. Oh, we were looking for her, we lost our feet, shouted, called, but where is it already there. The wolves must have bitten the poor daughter.

  The father began to cry with burning tears and went himself in search of his daughter: at least find the bones, pick them up and bury them humanly.

There had been no snowfall for two days, and following the old tracks of the skids he reached the pine tree where his wife had left his daughter to die. And he just found a rope, and next to him under a fir tree he saw an old coat, and felt boots. He pressed her old fur coat to his chest and wept bitterly. And this Uncle Frost took care of, put the girl's clothes there. Everything looked as if the wolves really pulled up and dragged away. The peasant from grief did not even notice that there were no traces of blood.

  Time passed, he mourned his missing child, but there was nothing to do.

  The New Year is coming soon and the Snow Queen and Uncle Frost, as always, prepared for it, collected gifts for poor children and orphans. And so the Snow Maiden had to walk through the forest at that time and tap the magic stick herself.

And one of these days, the king's son showed up in the forest to hunt with his retinue. The young prince, a dashing handsome guy with his friend, the son of an adviser and his retinue, came to the forest to frolic, shoot game and birds at the feast of the new year. This prince always competed with a friend in a dispute over who shoots accurately. And when one of them was the first, the second gave the first either a ring, or money, or something else - they bet on it. And the whole squad usually shot until it got dark, and they might not even take all the prey with them - they killed so many animals. In addition, the young men had fun with the fact that the loser's hair was dyed in different colors, that one day even the minister's son appeared in the palace with purple hair, for fun to the whole court.

The councilor's son teased the prince:

- Oh, yes, you shoot very poorly! See how I can and learn, - and shot, hitting right at the bump that hung high on a branch. And proudly hit his chest: - Seen?!

- Well, then let's shoot for money, since you're so accurate. I'll show you which one of us is the best shooter.

And both, each confident in himself, shook hands.

- Well, - the adviser's son chuckled, - I agree. Then in half an hour we meet at the same place and find out who will bring more game with them.

They decided and left.

The prince galloped, and his horse stumbled and the guy flew head over heels and fell into a pit, which was covered with snow. Hunters for wild animals dug it back in the fall and covered it with deadwood. And our prince fell into this trap. From above, from the branches, a thick layer of snow fell on him and he could not get out of this deep trap himself. There was almost no chance of salvation. He began to scream, call for help, but the snow and depth swallowed up his voice, even the echo remained inside the

pit. And when the prince fell, he hit his head so hard that after a couple of minutes he lost consciousness.

And the Snow Maiden, by the way, was walking nearby. She heard the ona hoot, the clatter of horses' hooves, and the barking of dogs in the distance. She walked there, but, before reaching the place where screams and laughter were heard, she stopped near a tall hundred-year-old pine. A horse stood there and neighed, and a huge hole gaped near it. She became a sorceress and therefore the events that happened ran before her eyes. The horse neighed and beat its hooves on the snow, calling its owner. The Snow Maiden was camouflaged with a thin layer, like a veil of fog, and covered with snow.

   -It was some hunters who set a trap for the beast: for deer or wild boar,- she sighed with regret. They didn't care who got there, but someone fell there and hit his head painfully.

The Snow Maiden, seeing the horse, came closer to him and saw a gaping hole in which lay a young handsome guy without feelings. His hat was pulled to one side and his curly hair fell over his forehead. His silky black hair only accentuated the beauty of his face. And thin gentle features said that he was of noble blood. The Snow Maiden blushed with excitement. From the cold, the wounded muttered, calling for help. When he sat there, he woke up a little and yelled again, began to call a friend for help, but his voice was hoarse and no one could hear him. Those were busy: at that time they were chasing a wild boar. The prince again fell into unconsciousness. The Snow Maiden tapped her staff and said:

   - Create a miracle: turn the ice into a step! - and from the wave of her hand, icy dust rose in the air and immediately an icy staircase appeared in the pit.

The prince woke up, as after a heavy long sleep and, seeing a ladder, he immediately climbed up it. The girl stepped back a little. As soon as the prince was at the top, the stairs immediately disappeared. He was surprised:

- Where's the stairs? Did it seem to me? How did I get out of there then? This is what I hit!

And then he saw the Snow Maiden aside, all sparkling in the sun in iridescent clothes. He looked at her

in surprise: he had never seen anything more beautiful before: so beautiful that she could not be told in a fairy tale or described with a pen. She was so embarrassed that her ruddy cheeks blushed like apples in the snow. Their eyes met. He looked over to where he had just been sitting and shuddered. He again looked at the stranger and no longer looked away from the beautiful maiden and wanted to touch her, but from her hand and from herself there was a breath of cold. And the prince recoiled. But still he asked:

-Who are you and how did you get here? - and he touched his head: - did I hit my head so hard? Do I see you in reality, or is it just me?

She said softly in a soft voice:

- I'm not allowed to talk to you.

- And who are you? What is your name?

The snow maiden did not answer. She turned around and walked away.

- When will I see you again? -the prince shouted after her.

And only her voice flew:

- In March, when there will be no snow left in the forest and snowdrops will bloom. Here at the same place.

And this sonorous tender voice sounded in his head. The prince trudged back with his horse and was perplexed, looking around and for the first time with surprise noticed the hitherto invisible enchanting beauty of the earth: he had never noticed such a winter landscape before.

- What is the beauty around? How did I not notice this before?! Everything is as beautiful as you, my stranger. Even the head is spinning with delight ... Oh, what fresh air!

Still hoping to find his ghostly beauty, he looked around: where are the traces of the girl, because she left, but left no traces. He thought: "I must have imagined all this," he touched his head, which was aching from a bruise, and felt for a huge bump. - What is it then? From the fact that he hurt his head and dreamed of all this? - he hit himself on the head and said: - No, I definitely hit! It's obvious that I got carried away.

But for some reason, her gentle voice continued to sound in his head, promising to meet at the same place in the spring. So it was all real.

While he was thinking and admiring the fabulous beauty, his thoughts were interrupted by an adviser with servants. A friend rode up to him with a retinue and across one horse lay a huge boar with fangs, through which fresh blood flowed onto the snow. Blood flowed from the wound and the white snow turned red.

- Where did you disappear to? And where is your game? - looked at him from all sides friend and grinned: - Lost?! And we shot a boar here.

- Ahh, yes, I lost ... - the prince breathed out, and his thoughtful gaze was fixed somewhere far away and his thoughts hovered in a completely different place. He didn't even react to the boar.

- And why are you so strange, some other become? - surprised one of the courtiers. To which the prince waved his hands and circled the air with them:

- Can't you see the beauty around? Just a fairy tale!

Someone ordered:

- We're going to the palace.

And the prince added:

- Enough game for us! There is no point in wasting too much.

Everyone looked at him in bewilderment and whispered:

- He became some sentimental.

   - Surprisingly, - a friend approached the prince, - I did not notice before that you felt sorry for someone. What happened to you?

   The prince shrugged. Then the chief archer rode up to them and asked loudly:

   - Well, shall we shoot again?

   -No, we already have enough game,- the prince sighed. -Get on your horse, let's go home.

   The prince could not stand it and on the way he told a friend:

- You know, I met the most beautiful girl here and fell in love. At the beginning, I fell into that hole and she pulled me out, or I got out myself, I don't understand.

   The friend laughed.

- Here you hit your head so hard, it already seemed that you were already in the forest beautiful girls imagining.

- No, really, I saw her.

- Where is she then, we didn't even find traces of her beautiful legs. Ha ha ha.

The prince scratched the back of his head:

-Hmm, I guess I really got it all wrong.

But the next day, the prince could not stand it, mounted his horse and galloped into the forest again, without even informing his father. One galloped off and wandered for a long time with his horse through the forest, hawked, called her, looked under the highest fir trees, kept trying to find her trace. But not that there was no presence, even her spirit, but he returned home with nothing. He became twisted, every day he began to yearn for her more and more, that he himself did not notice how, in his sadness, he began to spend more time alone in nature. Friends ceased to interest him, cruel hunting, he began to avoid all royal feasts, celebrations.

The king's father noticed that his son was somehow sad and asked:

- What is the reason for your turmoil?

The young man told his father. And the king loved his son more than life, patted him on the shoulder, was kind, affectionate with him and lamented that his son really injured his head. He decided then that it was time to marry his son. Yes, and the queen's mother was domineering, and had long wanted to marry her son to a neighboring princess - it hurt that girl to her liking - they were of the same character as her. Both in character were like two sisters. Yes, and from childhood, the children were friends, played together, got used to each other, no longer a stranger, so even they lived in the neighborhood. They will meet, it happens, the queen and that princess together and cannot talk enough, gossip, they will sort everyone out by the bones, discuss them. And the parents of the princess were only for intermarriage and unite both kingdoms in the future. So the poor prince had no choice, or rather, no one asked him. The queen, although a mother, did not pay attention to the change in her son's mood. It seemed to her that the engagement was the best way out of his sadness, so she decided to quickly marry her son to the princess and he would become content and happy. Everyone thought it was the best way out.

In the kingdom now there was only gossip about the upcoming wedding. The princess herself was crazy about him, she just waited, dreamed when she would become his wife as soon as possible. She even convinced both parties that it was better for her to settle on the eve of the wedding with her maids in the palace closer to the groom. The future mother-in-law was very happy about this, because she became the initiator.

   And the prince, having learned that they were going to marry him, was even more upset. The councilor's son came to tease him:

- Well, my friend, you will soon be seized, and you will forget us.

   - I don't want to marry her.

- Oh, my team, I recognize an old friend. You are my team! He patted the prince on the shoulder.

-Let's go to the forest,- the prince suggested, and after a few minutes they were already galloping there.

Remembering the face of the Snow Maiden, a smile appeared on his lips.

-Why are you smiling to yourself? - asked a friend.

- Look how the snow sparkles here.

- Yeah, - a friend noticed, - especially this year, it seems doubly beautiful, as if someone has tried especially for us.

- Well, someone added more shine and clean air, - and they laughed, spurred their horses and rushed off to the races.

Prior to this, the prince had even almost fallen ill, stopped going hunting, but still, with a friend, he now felt in the forest that this was the most suitable place to visit so that the longing would pass.

Then the horses stopped abruptly, began to beat with their hooves, snorted. The prince recognized this place.

- My horse smells someone. Who's here? he shouted, and the branches of the trees swayed, although at that moment there was not even a slight breeze.

The prince jumped off his horse and rushed there, and on the snow, hooked to a branch, in front of his eyes hung a small silver ring with an iridescent diamond. The prince gasped.

 - It's her ring! - and with trembling hands he carefully removed the ringlet from the branch, brought it to his eyes, then to his lips, kissed it, for this was proof that he had not imagined it.

 A friend came over. Without a word, the prince handed him the ring in his palm.

- Oh, my friend, well, you really got into trouble. And I didn't believe you.

 Together they went around all the spruce trees in the area, but again they did not find any traces, only a squirrel, shaking off the snow from a branch on their head, jumped away, and nearby, on a mountain ash, a bird pecked at frozen berries.

The Snow Maiden, waving her staff, became as invisible to everyone as Santa Claus, and simply watched them. And the heart, looking at the prince, beat faster. And when the prince came there, he disappeared into the forest every day. He took with him a bag of oats or cakes, threw them to the birds, walked through the forest and called his beloved.

In fact, she was always so close to the prince, he just did not see and did not know that she was watching him. She could not appear before his eyes again, they could not openly hold hands and walk together through the forest, admire its beauty, enjoy the singing of birds.

And out of longing for him, she furtively cried with pearly tears, and the squirrels ran up, caught them and collected them in a hollow. She hid her feelings from Uncle Frost so that he would not get angry, because she promised to help him until spring. But is it possible to hide something from him? As soon as she fell in love, her heart became hot and the Snow Maiden melted a little. Uncle Frost took pity on her and decided to change his condition: even then, so that she doesn't melt at all:

- I see, love has melted your kind heart. But I don't want to lose you, so I'm changing the condition: you can love him at a distance, but you shouldn't meet until spring.

- I agree, father. I don't want to lose you either.

And so she walked through the forest, grieved, yearned for her beloved, and tears rolled down from her eyes and became pearls. And nimble squirrels ran after her and collected precious stones, saved up for her dowry.

As soon as the prince received news from her, this silver ring, he believed that she was real and began to delay the wedding under any pretext until spring. And his bride was angry and did not understand why he was in no hurry to get married. Under any pretext, she resorted to him, invited him to all sorts of entertainment events, started long conversations. He was already pretty annoyed by her claims and he was just looking for an excuse to escape from her: either his friend came, or he urgently needed to hunt, because the game was over in the royal kitchen, then help his father, then a migraine suddenly broke out.

It's already March. Although the snow had not completely melted, the prince could not bear it any longer and hurried to the place of the appointed meeting. As soon as he began to pull on his boots, the bride entered the hall:

- Oh, where are you going? Can you take me with you?

- Yes, nothing special, I decided to take a walk through the forest with a friend. Girls don't belong there. There are many wild predatory animals there, - and as soon as he bent down to put on the second boot, a ring fell out of his breast pocket and rolled up to her feet. She quickly bent down and grabbed it:

- What an unusual ring?! Such a big diamond! - the princess exclaimed in surprise, even in her collection there was not such a large stone. - You cooked this for me?

The prince hesitated.

- Oh, yes, but it's too early now, I'll give it to you at the wedding, - and hastily snatched it from her.

But the confusion cast doubt on the princess:

- He's behaving strangely. It would be necessary to find out more about all this, - and, pretending to leave, she went to the stable.

The prince hoped that spring had finally come and that the forest beauty would already fulfill her promise. He jumped on a horse and therefore, without calling anyone with him, rushed into the forest. And the princess, who secretly followed his every step day and night, furtively saddled her horse and rode after him, keeping her distance so that the prince would not notice her.

She had noticed for a long time that the prince often went to the forest for no apparent reason, he didn't even bring a shot partridge from there. She suspected if he had a girlfriend there, with whom he secretly meets with everyone. And this case with the ring all the more prompted her to act, confirming her doubts.

- Ah! Where are you? - the prince called his stranger in that place by the pit. -Why don't you answer me, my love? I can't live without you.

-Who else does he call his favorite? I'm almost a wife, the kingdoms are almost united, and he runs into the forest to meet someone secretly?! Do not be this, otherwise I'm not me! - and, convulsively turning her horse, rushed headlong to the palace to complain to the queen.

The queen, seeing her future daughter-in-law in this form, rose from her chair in surprise:

- What is the matter with you, my child, why is your face distorted by such hatred? Who hurt you?

The princess, without answering, threw herself on her chest. The queen looked at the girl incomprehensibly, even stroked her head a little, trying to calm her down and stop her profuse tears. And the girl began to speak:

- The prince does not want to marry me because he has someone. He goes to meet her in the woods.

The queen drew back slightly.

- Are you sure about this? Maybe it's your imagination? Have you seen anyone with him?

She brightened up a bit:

- Not.

- Well then, wipe your tears and calm down. It's just pre-wedding girlish excitement. You imagined all this for nothing. You stood a little further away from him and could not hear his words or misunderstood.

The princess, having calmed down a little, went to her chambers, and the queen tensed:

- Without my knowledge, no one dares to do what he pleases, even my son!

And she sent heralds to all corners to announce that the wedding would take place in three days. There is nothing more to wait and postpone.

And at this time, the prince was still in the forest, at the place of the appointed meeting. He took out the ring of his beloved and pressed it to his chest for a long time, and the Snow Maiden stood invisible at a distance and did not dare to appear before his eyes. According to the conditions, not all the snow in the forest has melted yet, and therefore she could not become a simple girl.

When the prince returned to the palace, the dressers directly attacked him to take measurements from him for the solemn costume, which they had to have time to sew for the wedding ceremony. He tried to get away from them.

- What are you doing here? Why are you suddenly pestering me, why such haste? Let me get changed.

And the costumers interrupted each other:

- Your Highness, the wedding is in three days, we need to hurry to sew a camisole and a white shirt with diamond cufflinks, otherwise you have lost a little weight during the winter, the old measurements are no longer suitable.

At such news, the prin

- What wedding?! After three days?! Who decided so, I'm not ready yet!

- Your mother ordered.

Having pushed everyone in different directions, the prince rushed to his mother's chambers. Throwing open the door and not even saying hello, he shouted:

- Your Majesty, what do you allow yourself?! You're not getting married, I'm getting married! Why did you bring the wedding forward?

The queen extended her hand majestically and commandingly said:

- I am, after all, your mother and I decide when your wedding will be. We've already delayed her quite a bit.

Tears of hopelessness flowed from the prince's eyes: his own mother does not understand him. And with trembling lips he squeezed out:

- Not to be, not to be, - and, clutching his head, he ran out of his mother's chambers.

He did not want to return to himself and went to his friend. And along the way he came across fussy courtiers, servants carrying trays with gifts in their hands, with boxes of all kinds of things needed for the celebration. It seemed to the prince that he was going crazy: everyone around him was flickering, moving at lightning speed.

A friend was waiting for him at home:

- I knew you'd come. And the messengers have already arrived. I understand you perfectly, my dear

friend, but be patient, calm down. We have three more days left. Suddenly something will happen or we will think of something.

The prince returned to his room, took sleeping pills and fell into oblivion. All the next day he did not want to receive anyone and sat, closed, in his chambers. Various thoughts swirled in his head. But nothing came to mind. And the next day in the morning, the bright rays of the sun almost melted all the snow and only rare snow islands remained gray under the trees. Snowdrops grew during the night, coltsfoot blossomed, birds chirped happily, calling to different voices. In the garden, already early in the morning, the kids, the cook's assistants, were tumbling and frolicking. They plucked a young nettle on cabbage soup. The prince was especially fond of this dish, but this time he had no time for cabbage soup.

- This is real spring. Today I will definitely meet her there! - the guy exclaimed and ran to the stable for the horse.

But when he rode into the forest, the snow was still thick. It only melted noticeably in the sun. He still, hoping to meet the girl, rushed to the appointed place. His thoughts frantically swirled in his head: look for a way out, there must be one!

   He waited there for a solid three hours, but no one showed up. And the Snow Maiden at that moment was spending time with the Snow Queen and Uncle Frost.

   - Soon in this forest our dominance will end and we will have to leave for the polar ice until next winter.

The girl was bitter to part with her foster parents, but she understood that it should be so. She will now be able to see the prince, meet her father.

The prince returned home in deep sadness, where nothing awaited him but a hopeless marriage. His father comforted him as best he could.

   - Son, you'll get married and everything will be fine with you. You are having kids. We need strong and brave princes like you. And you have a good fiancee. See how he loves you. And the two states will already be as one. You look, money will increase in the treasury and our enemies will begin to be afraid to attack us.

But the prince did not feel better from his father's exhortations. But he did not dare to argue with his parents, realizing his royal share. He is the future ruler and is obliged to take care of the welfare of his state first of all.

   And then came the long-awaited day for the princess. Dressed with the help of maids in the most

expensive silks, she showed off in front of huge mirrors and already imagined how the prince would wrap her in his arms.

   In the morning, the prince was stuffed with cakes, like a small child.

- Open your mouth, my little chick, - mama shoved a golden spoonful of chocolate cream into his mouth.

-Well, mother, leave it, I don't want to,- he dodged, but the adamant mother persistently fed him piece after piece:

- Eat and get better, completely emaciated. Not good for a skinny prince to walk. Today you will become an adult man and must gain strength.

The cooks in the kitchen scurried back and forth, rattling pots, as if a feast was being prepared for the world. All the halls were decorated with luxurious roses, archideas, specially commissioned for this day, grown in Holland. The orchestra rehearsed the wedding march. The troubadours chirped on their violins. The dancers performed a variety of steps. The palace was seething with wedding preparations like chicken broth in a cauldron.

And the prince's heart ached incredibly to pain: is it really the end?! Now he will never see the forest maiden and will not even be able to dream of her. And his anguish tore at his chest so much that he lay down at the window and wept softly. His melancholy was so strong that it flew up to the forest and was transmitted, piercing with an arrow, into the chest of the Snow Maiden, and the girl shuddered, and her heart began to beat violently. She pressed her hand to her chest, exclaiming:

- Oh, uncle, I feel bad. I feel trouble with the prince!

- Yes, my dear, go, it's time.

-But the snow in the forest has not yet completely melted,- she looked around in fright.

Uncle jumped out into the street from the ice palace and hit the ground with his staff. The snow immediately melted, except for his palace. The Snow Maiden ran out and clung to his chest.

- Don't cry, baby, we're not parting forever. You need to hurry.

She turned into an ordinary girl, but remained just as beautiful and sweet. She missed her father, she knew that he came to the forest, looked for her, at least to bury the bones and cried, but now it was more important for her to find the prince. Uncle Frost whistled and a snow-white horse galloped to the whistle.

- Hold on, he'll take you wherever you want. Your instinct and loving heart will show you the way.

The Snow Maiden rushed straight to the place where she saved the prince and where she promised to meet him in the spring. But he wasn't there. She became even more worried and whispered to the horse to rush with all her might to the city and look for her betrothed there. Once on the city streets, she heard people say that the prince was being married today and was being led to the crown right now. She rushed to the central town hall, and there were crowds of people that it was impossible to get through people. The girl mentally asked Uncle Frost to magically send her through the crowd to look at her beloved with at least one eye, but Frost did not hear and she herself, leading the horse by the tie, tried to squeeze through. People pushed her away, threw her back, and then the crowd rejoiced:

- They're coming, they're coming! Prince, princess, king and queen! - and through the parting crowd along the road, sent by red poppies, prancing on a bay horse, a handsome prince with a sad face. And behind him in a gilded carriage rode an elegant, happy bride. Finding herself in the crowd of people, the

Snow Maiden looked longingly at the happy faces of kings and queens, the arrogant, graceful bride, and the beautiful sad groom.

   As soon as the girl saw her lover, her heart skipped a beat. And then she realized that this was the last time she saw him. He will soon get married and she will finally lose him. She looked at the prince with pity and began to cry.

And from her eyes tears splashed and flowed like a river, turning into huge mother-of-pearl pearls. Round, they rolled and clanged against the ground. Surprised exclamations were heard in the crowd:

   - Pearls! - and everyone rushed into the fray to pick up jewelry.

   The pearl rolled more and more. People standing nearby rushed into the fray to pick it up. The women squealed, someone stepped on their toes. Men scolded, crawling underfoot. Even children managed to snatch pearls and put them in their pockets.

The prince, hearing this absurd clamor, seemed to wake up from a deep sleep. And such a picture appeared before him: everyone was rushing about, crawling on all fours, hitting each other, tearing pearls out of their hands, showering each other with abuse. And among them stands a pale, beautiful girl, from whose eyes beautiful pearls roll. She stood looking at the prince. She stood alone and cried all the time, not paying attention to the crowd under her feet. For a moment they looked at each other, and only now the prince began to come to life and realized that it was she who was his forest Snow Maiden. The guy almost went crazy:

It's her, my love! At that moment, no one else in the world existed for them. They only saw each other.

They did not hear the bride screaming from the carriage.

She tried to get out, but her huge wedding dress interfered so much that she opened the door and fell out of the carriage, tangled and stepped on her magnificent dress in a hurry. The servants rushed to pick her up, shake her off. And the two father-kings, who were proud of the bride's carriage behind, stopped and only watched what was happening.

- What's going on here? - exclaimed, indignantly, the neighboring king.

  - I did not understand. But ... the girl is really good, - the father of the groom thoughtfully stroked his beard.

  The prince jumped off his horse and ran to her. She held out her hand to him.

  - It's me, my love!

  - Yes, my love, let's run faster!

And then her white horse arrived in time behind. The prince, without hesitation, grabbed him by the knot, seated the beauty on him, and jumped up himself. At that moment, the princess had already run up, holding the hem of her dress in an armful, and tried to grab the groom by the camisole. But the horse rushed forward and her outstretched arm hung in the air. Distraught, completely bewildered, she remained standing in the middle of the crawling crowd.

  Then the king and queen arrived in time for the dumbfounded princess:

  - Nothing, we'll catch up with them. Do not worry.

People, having collected full pockets of pearls, began to slowly disperse to their homes, quietly whispering about what had happened. Offended parents took their daughter home.

A loving couple arrived in the forest. They were greeted joyfully by Uncle Frost and the Snow Queen. Embraced them with tenderness.

- I will provide you with a crystal palace in the thicket of the forest, this will be our wedding gift to you.

And the Snow Queen had a magic ring, because with the help of it she instantly found herself here and there. She took them by the hand, rubbing the ring, and they all immediately found themselves in the most impassable part of the forest, where no human foot had set foot. Immediately, Uncle Frost waved his staff several times and created a crystal palace. And the lovers lived in it soul to soul.

The prince, not believing his luck, could not get enough of the Snow Maiden and every day talked about how much he loved her.

- Everyone convinced me that you were not there, and I already believed in it, that I almost got married. I always went to the forest to look for you. And every time I doubted whether you were real or I invented you.

- But I was a Snow Maiden, and I couldn't just appear in front of you. And I suffered from it. And the days seemed like months to me, because I was impatiently waiting for spring, when the spell would fall and I would become an ordinary girl again.

For a long time his father was looking for fugitives. And the friend said that the prince should be looked for in the forest and the king sent an army there. Everyone combed the whole forest, and found the crystal palace. The king was immediately informed. The queen almost died of anger, but when she heard that her son lived in a crystal palace and that they had countless jewels, she immediately calmed down:

-Hmm, curious, I would like to take a look at this palace.

And, without hesitation, they went there with the king, accompanied by his retinue. And when they arrived there to visit their son, seeing a happy beautiful couple, they were so amazed that the mother resigned herself to everything and did not interfere with their happiness anymore.

Immediately, Uncle Frost appeared with the Snow Queen, accompanied by a flock of squirrels, who brought chests of diamonds and pearls.

   - Here is the dowry, - Uncle Frost pointed to the treasures. - It was your daughter-in-law who cried so much, missing the prince.

   The parents were surprised, affectionately looked at the daughter-in-law, stroked both of them on the head, and the queen hugged her like a daughter: who else can boast that her daughter-in-law has such adoptive parents as Uncle Frost and the Snow Queen.

   So the parents of both accepted and the prince and his wife came to live in the palace with the king. After meeting with the lords of winter, when she was told that her daughter-in-law was like a daughter to them and they gave her so much treasure for her, the mother-queen fell in love with the girl at all.

So the Snow Maiden and the prince lived in two houses: the young couple either lived in the palace with their parents, or in the crystal palace, which never melted.

But the Snow Maiden did not forget her father either, she took him to live with her. When he found out that his daughter was alive and unharmed, he was very happy and jumped with happiness.

The Snow Maiden forgave her stepmother, she did not hold a grudge against anyone. If not her hatred for her stepdaughter, the girl would not have met her prince and such wonderful kind Uncle Frost with his icy, but such a good-natured wife. And the Snow Maiden did not do bad to her stepmother, and did not punish, because she is different and unlike her: she does not harm anyone. But she did not take her stepmother with her. Left her in that house and gave her a dowry for her stepsister.

So everyone lived in contentment and for the glory and prosperity of the state. The prince ruled the country together with his wife when the king-father retired. And every winter they visited Uncle Frost.

Humpback shoemaker

Once upon a time there was an old shoemaker with his son in a small village. The son was hunchbacked from birth and only beautiful blue eyes with lush dark long eyelashes adorned his face. Dark brown hair fell in waves over his shoulders. The whole village felt sorry for him and did not offend him, but they called him the Hunchback.

But the village was small, and therefore the father managed to do his work here, and the guy went to repair shoes in the city. There, in the market, he settled down near one wall, nailed shelves for tools so as not to interfere with others. And everyone who needed his services came to him. And sometimes he went on a call to take measurements from someone's legs for sewing new shoes. And wherever he went to repair or clean the shoes of the masters, he was often offended: who would not give him money for the work done, who would pay less than what was promised. And if he asks his own, they will kick him, and even shout that he ruined all their shoes. The guy would be offended, but he couldn't do anything. He will wipe away a tear and turn back to himself under a canopy in the workshop.

His father taught him his skills, but he did not teach him to read and write - there was not enough money even for food. And so it went year after year without hope and light.

Once a humpbacked shoemaker was sitting at his workplace and he was again short of money for repairs. The master wept out of resentment:

- Woe to me: no justice in life. No future, at least drown.

He hears two men talking behind him. One says to the other:

- You know, friend, there is a black castle almost in the forest. A sorcerer lives there and whoever comes to him for help, he helps everyone and all their wishes come true. Let's go and we'll go to him, because our life is not sweet.

- Is it safe? With us it will not be worse from this visit?

- Don't worry, everyone praises. And they even say that whoever pleases him, he will open the recipe for smelting pure gold. Will we get lucky?

They agreed to leave immediately. The shoemaker stopped crying and decided to follow them too. Goes and thinks:

- What if it's true? Could this be my chance to make a difference? So I'll take it and ask myself for

magical powers to punish my offenders. What are they all evil and bad. I need to teach them a lesson so that they respect the work of others and continue not to deceive.

He got up, gathered his tools into a knapsack, and followed the men.

The little hunchback did not hear their further conversation and kept thinking that it would only get better for him - after all, it doesn't get any worse.

In front of the castle they were enveloped in a thick dark fog. The petitioners were frightened and, holding their breath, not even daring to whisper, trudged to the entrance on shaky legs. And then, in front of their very nose, a massive gate opened and the guards let the travelers inside. And inside it was even worse. Horror gripped all three. They trudged behind the guards, silently looking at the black walls of the corridors in the semi-darkness, lit by rare torches. And so they followed the silent armored guards, shying away from their long flickering shadows. The flickering light of the torches partly illuminated their frightened faces, distorting their expressions beyond recognition.

The guards led the men up the spiral stone stairs to the top. They were launched into a separate damp room with a small high window just under the stream. Behind them, the door slammed shut and ominously ticked the lock. In a black corner, an owl suddenly hooted, demanding to tell him the reason for the visit.

And the Hunchback was led further along the corridor. The same black stone walls and wide slab floor lit the torches on the walls. The fire flickered ominously and the shadows reflected on the wall like terrible monsters, laughed and danced from the breath of the breeze emanating from those walking. Goosebumps of fear ran through the shoemaker's body.

At the entrance, the door opened by itself and the shoemaker entered a large dark round hall, or rather, he was pushed inside, where in the middle, with his back to the person who entered, the owner of this castle was sitting on a high black throne. The sorcerer snapped his finger and then the stove on which the chair was creaked, and the throne began to slowly turn to face the newcomer. Piercing black eyes, like those of a kite, stared at the guy, as if looking for a victim. The shoemaker cringed, feeling like a mouse in front of a huge bird of prey preparing to attack him.

The owner was large, dressed in all dark, with long shiny buttons on a satin cloak and the same shiny raven-colored hair. His big nose was piled up on a high-cheeked face, to which thick eyebrows, pulled down over eyes with a red tint, gave even greater severity and inflexibility.

He sat straight, arrogantly looking into space, and when the guy approached, he stood up and his black cloak touched the floor. He was of enormous stature, even taller than expected, with broad shoulders. The hunchback shuddered involuntarily.

One single window illuminated this gloomy hall with a strip of dim light. The pale moon in the black sky tried to seep into this gloomy lair, but the sorcerer waved his cloak like a wing and closed the window with himself.

A large cauldron was piled up in the corner of the wall, and some thick yellow-red mixture gurgled there. The magician silently led the visitor there and pointed to the brew:

- There is a golden night brewing. And why did you come? The guy just opened his mouth parched with fear:

- How is the golden night?

But the sorcerer chuckled.

- All strength and power is based on what is being prepared here at night.

The guy scratched behind his ear, trying to guess.

- I ... this ... I wanted to ask here ... - the guy tried to gather his thoughts.

- You can not answer - I already know. Disadvantaged people like you come for money, for fame, or to take revenge on someone. I guessed?

- You guessed it, - the shoemaker stuttered.

-Ha-ha-ha,- the sorcerer laughed dully. - I knew you would come. I've been waiting for you for a long time.

- Y-yes?

- Say what you want most of all: to take revenge on the offenders or to get rich?

The humpbacked man thought, not knowing what to choose, but then his side ached from a recent kick. And tears welled up from his eyes.

- Punish offenders.

- All right, it will be done. Would you like to get both?

The boy's eyes sparkled with hope.

- Of course I would!

- Look, - and the magician pointed to the gurgling cauldron. - Gold is brewed here.

-But is it green?! -exclaimed the shoemaker.

- Haha. That's when it boils and hardens, then it will shine so that, looking at it, people's eyes will go blind.

The humpbacked man looked without blinking at the cauldron and the large bubbles in it.

-I'll teach you how to cook it,- the mage continued in a deep voice.

- You will become a different person, powerful, omnipotent, beautiful and without a hump. But you will stay in my castle. You won't need anything. And at night you will turn into a fierce ferocious werewolf, you will visit everyone who deserves it, you will instill fear in the whole district, and so you will take revenge on your offenders.

The shoemaker was talking to himself:

- This wolf-like creature will be me, and I am he. I will scare people. And in the afternoon, as usual, I will go to the market and buy what I want.

The sorcerer read his thoughts and nodded in agreement:

-        Correctly. You can even run and go to your village in any guise to visit your father, but you have no right to stay there even a single night.

- And how can I explain my transformation to dad? - looked up at the gray face of the sorcerer - it was also impenetrable, without emotions.

- But the father does not recognize you, he will think that you are a new friend of his son. You can even visit him in the guise of a werewolf, if you don't scare the old one to death, - and he laughed. - Have you changed your mind yet?

-No, I want to,- the Hunchback straightened his chest.

-        Well. All this will give you strength, but in return for such a life, you must give your soul to the devil. Do you also agree now?

- And why do I need such a soul, if I constantly have nothing to wear, put on shoes, then my stomach is empty for several days?! - all the resentment accumulated over the years burst out. - Yes, they beat and offend me all and sundry.

-Say yes at once, and we will seal the contract with your blood.

 The hunchback held out his hand:

- Cut.

Fresh scarlet blood dripped into the cauldron from the incision.

- Did you think well? - continued to interrogate the sorcerer. - You still have time to refuse.

- And what good do I have now - nothing, - the shoemaker reasoned and waved his hand.

- So, you agreed, - with an inner smile, the sorcerer cut his ring finger and attached an imprint to what was written on parchment.

The humpbacked man did not know how to read, and therefore he blindly trusted the charms, firmly deciding to take revenge on people for his torment and humiliation.

The sorcerer ran his hand over the head and shoulders of the shoemaker - he straightened up and the hump instantly disappeared, leaving in growth. The shoemaker stood tall and handsome. Instead of a freak - an attractive young man.

-Now take a look at yourself in the mirror.

- Where is it? - the guy tried to make out in the semi-darkness, and then a large mirror appeared in front of him in his entire height. He gasped: from the depths of the room, in a mirror reflection, it was not the former shoemaker, but a young unfamiliar handsome man who looked at him with wild surprise.

-        Who is it?! - Humpbacked put his index finger at him and the handsome man did the same.

-What, you looked in the mirror and didn't recognize yourself? -mage chuckled.

- Is it me? - the guy turned to the sorcerer, trying to realize the miracle.

-        As you see. I kept my word. And later you will witness your other changes.

The guy turned back to the reflection and froze in a clear smile, not believing his eyes: a beautiful, tall, happy young man with a white-toothed smile was looking at him from the mirror.

-Y-yes,- the boy stammered.

And so, from that moment, his new life began in the black castle of the sorcerer.

Until the early evening he slept, at midnight he turned into a ferocious-looking werewolf and ran around the district.

On the very first night, he ran to the house of his last offender, went into his bedroom, pulled the sleeping man out of bed and growled:

- Where is my payment for boots

- What boots, what money? I don

- What boots, what money? I don sleepy eyes with fear, squealing and dodging, vainly trying to escape from the strong paws of the beast.

- Remind you what money you didn't pay for my work? How did you repay me?

  Instead of answering, the werewolf kicked him with his paw with such force that he flew up to the very ceiling, shouting "awww!" and calling for help. The wolf did not answer, growled and rushed off into the forest.

The next morning, waking up with the cries of the first rooster, the shoemaker came to the market, looked at his empty place where he used to work, and was sad: how, however, life is changeable. Out of habit, he almost sat down at his workplace, but he caught himself in time, because he didn't even take his tools with him. And then he heard third-party speeches about himself:

- Where's the hunchback? He was so good at mending shoes!

-Yes, I got it cheap.

-I'm sorry, where did he go?

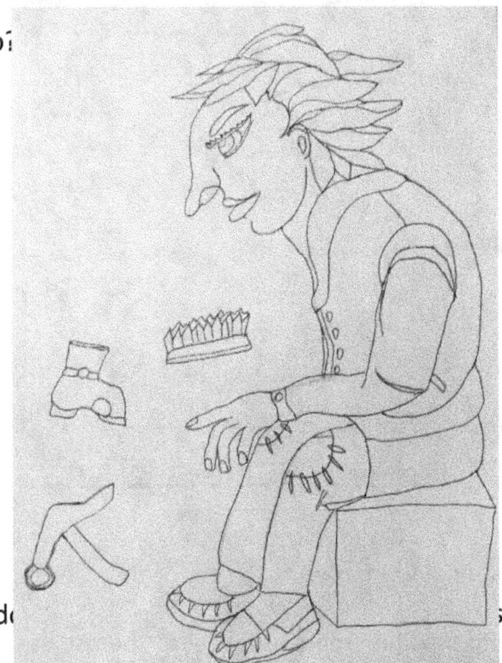

- My shoes are torn, but I do... ...sive, and they don't do quality work either.

The young man already shed a tear:

- Me, means appreciate? I thought only everyone hates, - the shoemaker's chest skipped a beat.

And then his thoughts were interrupted by a noise behind him. The guy turned around. A crowd gathered behind and someone called them to the house of a merchant, who had been staying with a werewolf at night.

- What happened to him?- some asked with curiosity.

- The werewolf showed up. He came tonight, - others replied.

The crowd hurried to the scene, and the merchant, taking advantage of such an unforeseen event, had already slaughtered his goat, smeared all the walls in the house with its blood, refurbished all the furniture, hung the skin on the gate, and threw the hooves into the garden. And now he invited the people to look at the work of the paws of the miraculous villain for a fee.

- Come see what the werewolf has done! He pulled up my goat, hung the skin on the gate, threw away the horns, the hooves separately, and the meat ... he ate all the meat, - and involuntarily stroked his bulging belly. - And with blood, look how he smeared all the walls with his claws? I barely survived!

- What a horror! - people groaned and paid him money to see for themselves.

- What a horror! - people groaned and paid him money to see for themselves.

- And how he beat me up, threw me under the ceiling! These are the bruises he left, - he showed the only true proof of his words.

- Come on, come into the house. Just for a nominal fee.

And for a small fee, the curious, with their mouths open, threw coppers into his open hem of his shirt, eager to see what was there. And everyone himself imagined the horrors of the past night.

The guy went inside and threw him a coin of pure gold - the merchant almost choked. Greedily grabbed a coin and hurried to try it on the tooth.

- Who is this generous fool? I haven't seen this before. Foreigner, probably.

Crossing his arms over his chest, the guy walked around the house and shook his voice:

- Well, talker, ah yes rogue. He even made money from it. Well, I'll teach you a lesson, you bastard.

And that same night he broke into his house again. The merchant hasn't gone to bed yet.

By candlelight he sat at the table and recounted with pleasure the heap of money earned during the day, muttering:

- That's the profit! I earned so much in a day without even going into my store! Oh, yes, well done!

And then an ominous animal roar sounded behind him:

- Ah, do you count other people's money? Decided to make money on human naivety?!

The merchant jumped up in his chair. The wolf grabbed him by the scruff of the neck and began to shake him:

-I'll shake the whole spirit out of you if you still grind with your tongue. Remember: not a word more, not a half a word about the fact that I came to you, and not a drop of lies to anyone, otherwise I'll drink your blood, bite it,- and with these words he threw him to bed.

And the merchant buried himself in a thick blanket and shook there with fear that even the bed was shaking and banging against the wall like Morse code.

The werewolf scooped up all the coppers in the bag prepared by the merchant, tied it up and ran out of the house, leaving only his gold coin gleaming on the table - a reminder to the merchant that he should not forget to keep his promises, and about himself, about his coming.

The next day, a crowd of onlookers came to look at the traces of the monster, and the merchant with a cloth sat near the door and sadly wiped the traces of blood:

- Where's the werewolf? - disgruntled spectators shrugged.

- That's it, the show is over. No one came and will not come again, - the merchant sighed, regretting and shedding tears that he would no longer be able to earn easy quick money by deceiving visitors.

- Oh, how is it! -dissatisfied voices were heard.

-We came here from far and wide to look at this.

-Enough, everyone go home,- grumbled the merchant.

And onlookers, not having received what they promised, left, muttering under their breath:

- Just a waste of time. Whether he is bad.

The former shoemaker watched from afar, and was pleased that he stopped the greedy merchant. And the next morning the guy got enough sleep and came to the market. He approached a lonely woman who sold wild flowers every day, but few people took them. The humpbacked man had known this unfortunate widow with many children for a long time. He always repaired her and her children's shoes for free, sometimes even replacing them with newer ones.

Now she piercingly beckoned passers-by, holding out forget-me-nots, gladioli, daisies. Nobody paid attention to her. The shoemaker approached her and placed a heavy suede bag full of money in front of her nose. The woman lifted her head and blinked. The eyes filled with tears.

- Why so many? Even all my bouquets are not worth that much! This is many times more!

- I don't need your flowers. Sell them on. And this is for your children, feed and clothe them.

He turned around and walked on, but she could not believe in a miracle. And she called after the already receding figure:

-Thank you, good young man! - and raised her hands to the sky, rolling her eyes: - Oh Lord, Holy God, thank you! You have heard my prayers. I asked you for this for so long and you sent me this young man, your angel.

And so the shoemaker went around all his offenders, having taught them in full, sometimes being an unknown young man, sometimes being a nightmare. After that, his soul felt warmer, as if a weight had been lifted from his shoulders.

His father was all worried: there is no son for a day, there is no other. The old man burst into tears, wondering where the poor thing had gone:

- Did I offend him, or did negligent clients beat my son?

He questioned his acquaintances. With the last money he went to the city to the market to find out about his son. The people sympathized with him, even those who used to be rude to the Hunchback:

- Yes, he was a good guy, he did his job diligently, he would not say a bad word. Pity him, where did he disappear to? We worry ourselves.

The father returned home completely saddened, and just then someone knocked on the door, interrupting his sad thoughts. The old man opened. A tall, handsome stranger stood in the doorway.

- Who are you, young man, what do you need?

The young man wanted to rush to hug his father, but he restrained himself in time.

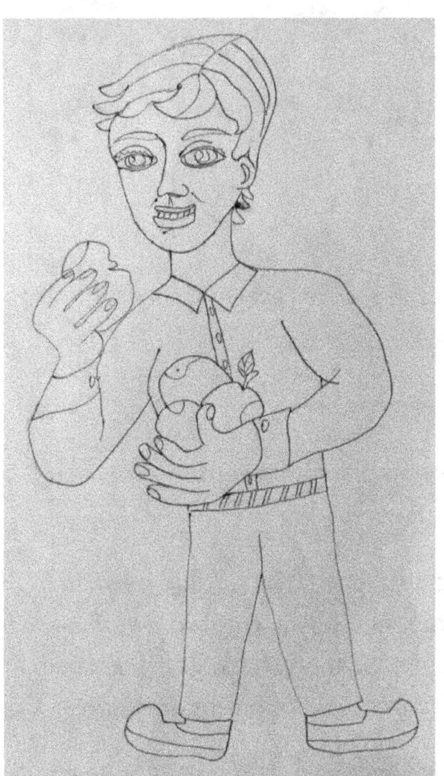

- I'm from your son.

-        And what happened to him? Do you know where he is?

-Yes, don't worry, he's fine.

-Tell me,- the old man grabbed him by the sleeve and dragged him into the house. He sat down on a stool.

- He's really good. An important nobleman saw what a skilled craftsman he was and hired him to work in the palace. He pays him well, and therefore your son asked me to tell you, - with these words, he handed his father a heavy bag of money.

-Why didn't he come himself?

- He is very busy with work. Many orders were received: shoes, boots to sew. When he is free, he will definitely visit you.

The old man burst into tears, not believing his luck:

- My son, let me at least hug you for his place. You lightened my soul, - and gently pressed the young man to his chest.

That same night, the villagers were awakened by a terrible howl. In fright, everyone jumped out with a pitchfork into the yard, into the street and saw a huge werewolf in the middle of the square. He stood and, in the light of the full-faced moon, beat his chest, uttering a piercing roar. And then he tossed them a huge bag. And gold coins scattered from it in different directions.

- This is all for you, for the good of the village! - he roared, got up on all paws and rushed off into the darkness of the forest.

People abandoned pitchforks, rakes, axes and rushed to collect gold.

- Oh, thank you!- they shouted after him.

- What only huge wolves we have not seen, but this, with burning blue eyes, for the first time!

- Yes still such kind and generous!

- He can talk!

 In the morning, the construction of new houses for the poor, the repair of cattle sheds and festive fun began.

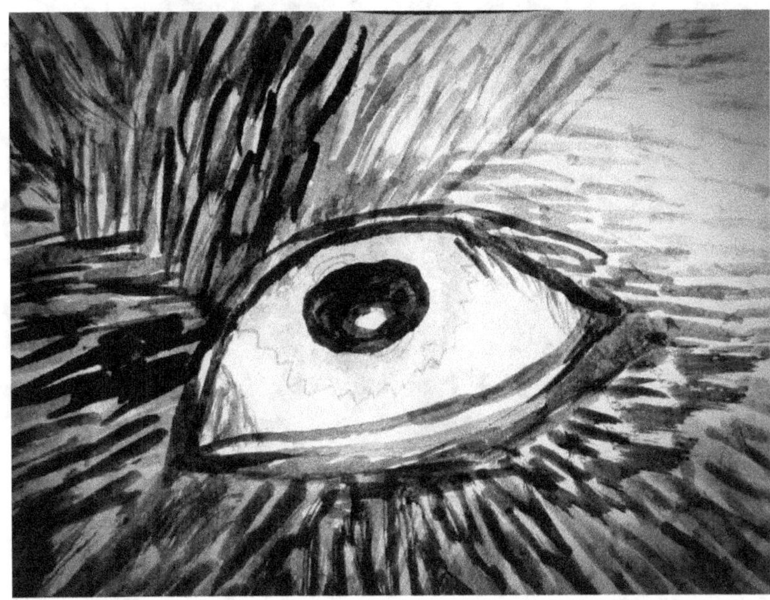

In a month, the shoemaker learned how to boil gold and mint coins, making them in chests and distributing them to poor people, learned to write and read. During the day he often went to the market in the city, and at night he wandered around the forests and villages.

One day at the fair he saw a beautiful girl: poor in torn shoes, she stood aside and sold sweets. He timidly approached her and put a handful of gold coins on the counter and said quietly:

- I'll sew you boots, I need to take measurements. Give me your leg. The girl blushed, lowering her eyes in embarrassment and not daring to move:

- Ah, me? - she was surprised and could not utter a word: she liked him so much, especially his blue, affectionate, big eyes.

After a moment's silence, she nevertheless asked:

- And who are you? Why are you giving me so much money? What's the reason?

- And I just liked you very much.

He bent down and, without touching her leg, ran his hand through the air and stood up embarrassed. He liked the saleswoman so much that he instantly fell in love with her and could not look away. So they stood for a long time in embarrassment, not daring to utter another word, and only secretly exchanged glances.

The girl sold candies, gingerbread, cakes and cream tubes. Parents with children came up and bought sweets, but her earnings were not enough for a hearty meal or warm clothes, because she was an orphan and worked for a rich confectioner who paid her for day miserable pennies.

And then the shoemaker approached her, having heard from afar her call to try new goodies. The boy's thin voice brought them out of their stupor:

- And give me, please, a red cockerel on a stick. The numbness passed and the girl reached for the candy. The boy held out a coin, but the shoemaker removed his hand:

- You don't need money.

- How not to? - the boy was surprised.

- And today I treat everyone! -The shoemaker's face lit up with a wide white smile.

The boy jumped for joy and rushed off to boast to his friends. Immediately a bunch of kids rushed to ask for candy. The saleswoman only had time to distribute left and right. And after half an hour all the sweets were distributed, and on the counter there was a weighty money bag.

- You didn't say who you are? - not so embarrassed, the girl asked the patron.

The boy looked at her with a wide smile.

- I'm Arthur, and what's your name, beautiful pie-woman?

Her cheeks flushed and she almost sang:

- Linda.

-        What a beautiful name.

-        Thanks. Your name is great too.

- Can we take a walk along the embankment? -he suggested.

The girl spread her hands

-        Unfortunately I can not. I need to take the proceeds to the owner of the shop and warm up a
bit.

Arthur again saw her shifting from one foot to the other in her worn-out shoes.

The next day, the shoemaker brought her warm boots, because it was already late autumn. The girl was
delighted, put her leg, fragile as porcelain, and, embarrassed, said sadly:

I can't thank you enough for such a priceless gift!- she gasped. - I'm an orphan.

-But I don't need anything,- answered the shoemaker. - The fact that you are in this world, so kind, is my
award. If I made you a little happy, then I'm very glad about it.

-Thank you very much,- she sang again in her honeyed voice.

- Today your feet will not freeze and we will be able to walk along the embankment.

Linda agreed, but was embarrassed, thinking that he was a prince in disguise.

On the way, he bought her flowers from a widow he knew. And finally, the girl dared to ask:

-How did you guess my shoe size? Such comfortable boots. Where did you buy them?

- I made them myself.

- Did you sew it yourself? -She even stopped in surprise. - Can you sew shoes?

-Of course, I'm a shoemaker,- he smiled. And my father is a shoemaker. He taught me this from childhood.

- And I thought ... - the girl began to talk about her assumptions about his origin, but then happily waved it off: - So he is not a nobleman, not a noble swaggering prince. He is a simple guy just like me! How cool! So we are equal! And he is so handsome, like a real prince. What I need.

 And they, holding hands, went for a walk around the city. And they felt so good with each other that they didn't even need words, as if they had known each other forever.

Every day they walked for hours. They ate ice cream, delicious lamb in a tavern, with hot cakes. In the morning he put a bag of gold coins on the counter, she distributed sweets for free to everyone in a row, gave money to the owner of the shop to go for a walk with Arthur.

And one day he didn't come. Arthur went to visit his father, but Linda did not know about it and became worried. And then it dawned on her:

- And where does he get so much money every day? He's just a shoemaker! Something doesn't fit here.

She tried to draw different conclusions, deduced all sorts of assumptions in her mind, and she became scared of them:

- And who is he really? He is a stranger to me. I don't know where he lives, we haven't seen his father. Is he deceiving me? Maybe he is a thief or a hired killer? Maybe I loved him for nothing? Or maybe he is some kind of prince, but he hides from me. Or already married? Oh my God! - the most terrible thoughts climbed into her head, stirred her heart.

She clutched at her chest, her breath caught:

- But even so, I can't leave him: I love him so much and I'm afraid to lose him! But let the bitter truth be better than the sweet lie. If he is cheating on me? I won't survive this,- bitter thoughts, one after another, climbed into her head.

And the next day, Arthur reappeared and, after walking along the embankment, said goodbye to her, leaving her a bag of gold:

- With this money, build yourself a house with a high fence, surround it with a deep moat filled with water, so that no one can offend you. I'll bring you even more gold tomorrow - I'm rich, don't worry.

But Linda pulled away.

- My dear, forgive me, but you know, bad thoughts creep into my head and do not give me rest. You said you were a shoemaker. But where do you get such huge money?! Even the most skilled famous royal shoemakers don't have that kind of money. Be honest, are you deceiving me? Are you a prince?

- Oh, no, dear, - embarrassed Arthur. - I'm not a prince at all and not at all as handsome as you think I am. I'm really the shoemaker's son. And very soon I will introduce you to my father.

-But then where does all this gold come from?

-And I'll tell you this too. Give me time. I will never deceive you or leave you.

Thoughts were confused and swarming in her head. She understood that in any case she would not be able to stop loving him, but could she accept the truth? And tears flowed from her beautiful eyes.

Arthur took a silk handkerchief out of his pocket and began carefully wiping her wet cheeks.

-I promise I will never hurt you. I love you very much. I have no one in this world more dear than you. Don't cry dear. You are mine forever and I am yours no matter what happens.

-And I love you,- the girl mu[illegible]er.

He began to visit her every day and they could no longer live without each other. The girl decided to completely trust him, because she loved him with all her heart. And so she agreed to wait until Arthur could explain to her the appearance of gold and introduce her to his father. With his money, the saleswoman, having hired the best workers, built a castle, so beautiful, to the envy of everyone, and hired guards.

When she asked if he had parents, Arthur remembered his father: how is he doing alone in the village? He gave him money last time, but the old man is no longer young and his health is not the same. And so the next day the shoemaker asked the sorcerer to let him go early to his father. He looked around the student with a piercing look and said with a whistle:

- So it's time for you to turn into a werewolf.

-I'll be in time for everything,- the guy wanted to justify himself, but the magician interrupted him:

- I relied on you, your hatred for offenders. You had to be furious and go around villages and cities at night, frighten and kill people. And you, miserable shoemaker, did not cope with my tasks, fell in love with the saleswoman and all your resentment and hatred towards people disappeared. You're throwing gold left and right!

- Forgive me, but I never wished death and severe suffering on my enemies. I just wanted to teach them. So don't expect bloody massacres from me.

And with these words, he turned around and, without looking back, headed for the exit.From such disobedience, the sorcerer shook all over with anger and hissed:

-Then it won't be as you wish. I will teach a lesson to all who dare to oppose me.

Evening came and the shoem[...]orm of a terrible werewolf. His red eyes burned like candles, and[...]erily and he looked like a huge wolf with huge paws. He reared up like a gorilla and growled. Seeing such a terrible monster, people in the village fainted, preparing for death, and instead of reprisals against them, he again threw gold coins at them, continuing his way to his father's house.

The old shoemaker was sitting on the porch, repairing shoes by the light of a dying candle and grieving for his son, when he suddenly raised his head from the screams of his neighbors and saw a werewolf approaching him. He gasped and crossed himself, closing his eyes and thinking:

- Lord, protect me and my hunchback from evil spirits! - and then other thoughts overwhelmed fear: concern for the failed child: - Where did he go, my son? He has been gone for three months already, - and suddenly his heart sank: - Why does the monster have the eyes of his son?

At that moment, the werewolf threw three bags of gold coins to the shoemaker and disappeared. The old man opened his eyes and looked down in surprise: he had a fortune in the hem of his apron. He was surprised and the neighbors who came to him also looked at the shoemaker with gaping mouths.

And after that day in the village they lived so happily and in abundance that they repaired all their houses, cellars and stables, bought new cattle, poultry and praised the wonderful werewolf. They were no longer afraid of him and bowed to him, leaving treats for him when he again came to the village to give them gold.

Meanwhile, the devil appeared in the black castle and yelled at the sorcerer:

- Hey you, miserable warlock, whom did you slip me? This shoemaker turned out to be with a good soul and cannot harm people! Then you yourself turn into a werewolf instead of him, harm everyone and let people think that he did so many troubles, and they themselves will take revenge and kill him. If you do not do this, then I will take your soul from you, and I will give you to people to be torn to pieces.

The sorcerer got scared and turned into a werewolf.

He rushed to the village to tear to shreds the headman, the most respected long-liver in the village, in order to turn the people against Arthur the werewolf. And as soon as he managed to tear off his thick jacket - grandfather was always cold, so he dressed more tightly, which saved him from deadly claws. The old man yelled with all his might, and then people with pitchforks and axes jumped out to the old man's cries for help, and wanted to pounce on the monster. But he turned sharply and jumped with ease over a two-meter fence, only once turning around and flashing at them with his huge red eyes, burning in the darkness like torches. People followed where he ran, chasing him with screams and hoots until he disappeared into his black castle. And the inhabitants decided to put an end to the werewolf, gathering together all the surrounding villages.

They returned to the village. And the grandfather moaned barely alive with fear, grunting from scratches and regretting the torn sheepskin coat. The neighbor's doctor examined him and announced:

- The wounds are not deep, recovering.

- Thank God, he will live, - the villagers crossed themselves.

Who did this to him? - Surprised examined the wounded doctor. - There is no such wild animal.

- And it was not an ordinary animal. Beast: Werewolf! - told him vying with each other.

And the sorcerer at that time could not sleep off, nervously giggled and worried about how to report to the devil:

- So will it go, my Lord? The people will now take up arms against the hunchback. Are you happy with me now?

From the dungeon came a loud voice:

- Am I satisfied? Are you kidding me? You didn't do anything, you couldn't even cope with the weak grandfather. Keep working, coward and clumsy.

As soon as dawn broke, the people of the whole village and adjacent villages began to go out in all weapons: some with pitchforks, some with shovels or rakes. Even children took with them sickles and hoes.

-Time to kill this bastard! -the men shouted.

- Get rid of the werewolf! -the women shouted.

- Stab him with a pitchfork! - squealed the kids.

And the whole indignant crowd went to the black castle to kill the werewolf. The whole district roared, dogs barked and howled in time with them, smelling blood in advance.

And already on the way to the castle they began to be enveloped in a thick dark fog with a pungent smell of sulfur. Superstitious fear followed him. The people began to exchange glances, cross themselves, clinging to each other:

- It smells like hell in here! - someone exclaimed loudly and everyone instantly froze.

And the fear began to grow with such a powerful force that it turned into panic. And with squeals and shouts, people rushed into the loose. This was the end of their failed trip to the werewolf castle.

In the morning everyone went to the church to consult with the priest, telling about what had happened.

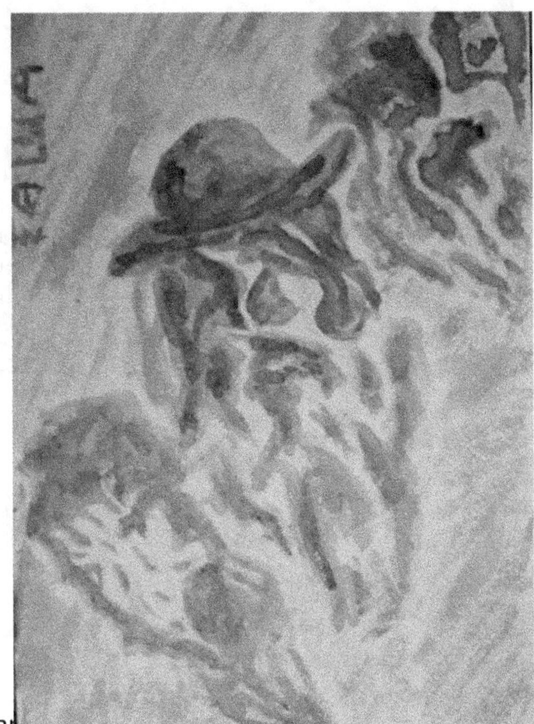

-        What to do? How can we overcome this wickedness?

- Yes, this castle has a gloomy reputation for a long time. Its entire history is shrouded in darkness. No pope, no king, no God himself set foot there. Nobody can beat him. And here I'm definitely not helping you. Read prayers - God help you, - and with that he left.

The men scratched their heads.

- Yes, we will have to lock ourselves up at night and not go out in the evening after dark. We cannot deal with it on our own.

And the Enchanter, getting even more angry with the Hunchback, decided to take revenge on him and, turning into a werewolf, ran to Linda that same night to bite her. The shoemaker also felt something was wrong, and, without hesitation, rushed after him.

And when he was about to grab and tear his beloved to pieces, the shoemaker also turned into a werewolf, attacked from behind and wounded the sorcerer so that he howled and ran away, not expecting a reciprocal attack. But in the end, the villain managed to scratch the girl. She staggered and almost fell - the shoemaker picked up to support her. Linda looked into his eyes and immediately understood from their expression that this was her lover, and lost her senses.

The beast put the girl on her back and carried her to his father. He ran foaming at his mouth, afraid that something might happen to her. He ran without stopping all the way to the house. Knocking down the door, at full speed threw the wounded woman on the bed and shouted to the old man:

- Dad, take your future daughter-in-law! Call the doctor, she's hurt, she needs help!

Dad was stunned when he recognized the voice of his son in the monster calling him dad. Moreover, the werewolf ordered to help his daughter-in-law. The old man bulged his eyes, opened his mouth and quietly, silently slid down the wall, emitting only a quiet whistle of amazement.

- And I have no time, I have to catch a real werewolf, - and, with a roar, jumping out, he ran to the black castle with only one thought to kill the sorcerer.

Then his father's eyes dimmed, his brain began to boil: what, is there another werewolf? Is that a toothy monster, a fake werewolf? And is he my son? How is this possible?!

As soon as Arthur jumped out, his father hesitantly stood up, looked around and quietly approached the girl, and carefully began to examine her delicate features. It seemed that the girl was not breathing - she was so pale.

- Oh my God, what a beauty! - exclaimed the old man and forgot about the werewolf. "Is she really going to be the wife of my freak?..." and, without finishing, he covered his mouth with his hand. - What a miracle! He flopped down on the floor in confusion.

And then, like a whirlwind, an even larger size, with a bared mouth, with bloody fangs and with red burning eyes, another snarling werewolf flew into the house. Without looking at the old man, he grabbed the girl from the bed and was gone.

The old shoemaker sprawled on the floor without a word, and so until morning he looked at the ceiling, digesting in his mind what it was at night.

- There was a beauty and there is no beauty. The monster came, brought her. The second came - took her away. What, am I nuts?

So he digested this porridge, not knowing how to tell his neighbors about it. In the morning he was completely confused and was about to tell a completely different story. But, in order not to go astray and gain courage, he grabbed a stack, crawled out on all fours to check if there was another werewolf outside.

After making sure that no one was there, he went to the neighbors to tell what had happened to him.

Arthur ran all over the forest, looking for the sorcerer, but, not finding him, returned to the castle. He flung open the gates and rushed inside, already smelling by scent that the sorcerer was here. The Black Throne had its back turned to him, just like the first time. The owner of the castle sat on it as the ruler of the world. Arthur wanted to pounce on him from behind, but the slab turned to face him with a creak and the shoemaker saw that at the very feet of the sorcerer lay lifeless, pale Linda. Arthur's heart sank at the sight of her, and he braked sharply, leaving deep streaks of claws in the floor. And holding his breath, he looked first at her, then at the sorcerer, trying to predict his reaction. At the same time, his brain was in full swing at work on how to get out of this situation as a winner, and without harming his beloved.

Here the sorcerer laughed with a hearty laugh and raised his leg over her:

- I'll crush her in an instant. Look!

- No, stop!

- Why did I give you magical powers and taught you how to cook gold? So that you do evil for the glory of the Devil. We even signed an agreement. And what are you doing? Giving away gold to miserable peasants. You use all your power for the benefit of people, but you must use it against them: you must rob, kill, destroy their homes.

And poor Arthur stood in front of him in complete confusion: indeed, he had violated the contract. But then he remembered that initially he wanted to punish only his offenders, and not all people.

-To be mean and cruel is not for me,- answered the shoemaker. -I am terminating my contract with you. Take your arcane tricks, your gold, your werewolf power. I don't need any of that, as long as you don't touch her.

The sorcerer removed his foot and laughed again:

-She's going to die anyway, why am I still going to mess with her.

He put forward his hand with a rod and exclaimed:

- Be yourself again!

At the same instant, Arthur turned into the former Hunchback, short, with tousled hair. And he immediately rushed to his beloved, lifted her up and tears dripped onto her face:

-Don't die, love! I am nobody without you. I am ready to give my life for you.

From his hot tears, she woke up and smiled weakly:

- Darling, why didn't you open up to me earlier and tell me who you are, I would still love you.

- Yes, how could I? Look at me, pathetic creature, I have a huge ugly hump. You wouldn't even look in my direction. And even if I did, I would bore you. You would have turned away, left me, and that would have been an even worse blow for me.

-Don't say that,- she slowly closed her eyes in exhaustion. Life came out of her.

- No, don't leave me!

Then the devil himself appeared from the black darkness of the dungeon and spoke in a muffled bass:

I will revive her, but in return you must give your soul to me.

- I agree to everything! - the guy exclaimed in despair. - Let me die, only that she lived!

But she wasn't dead yet, and she heard voices. She opened her eyes and groaned softly:

-I can't live without you either. Don't agree. You have a pure soul. Never sell it to the devil. It's the worst thing you can do. Without a soul, I won't need you either.

-But I can't let you die.

- And you let me, so it will be better. I can't live after such a sacrifice. I will end myself.

The devil only grinned at their eloquent speeches.

- Enough here for you to portray love dramas - I'm already sick of listening to you and your lamentations! I'm tired! Get down to business quickly. Are you giving me your soul or not?!

- Take it, it's yours! -The humpbacked man jumped up and opened his chest.

- Wow! - roared the devil and spun like a whirlwind: - I don't need this one! I came for the vile, worst, treacherous little soul. You promised me this! - turned to the sorcerer. - And what did you slip me? You failed my task! For this, I take your soul and turn you into a vile rat.

The devil hit the villain on the head with an iron staff and the wounded sorcerer began to decrease in size until he turned into a fat gray rat. She stood on her hind legs and began to squeak loudly, indignantly.

- Here, take your little rat soul! - the devil thundered in a terrible voice and threw a small ball of steam to the rodent. - Now you will definitely serve me regularly, doing dirty tricks to people.

A hoarse laughter of evil spirits was heard throughout the castle. And the sorcerer squealed even louder in response, never realizing that he was already a rat. But then, out of nowhere, a huge red cat ran out, bent, bristling, in an arc, preparing to jump. His fur stood on end. Only now did the sorcerer realize that he had become a rodent. And at the same moment he darted into a hole, and the cat, jumping after him, crashed into the wall.

The demon whirled around with a howl and began to disappear under the collapsed floor. Arthur shouted:

- Where are you? You promised to save Linda?!

The devil shouted so loudly that the whole earth trembled:

- I can't take your soul: it doesn't suit me! - and with a cackle fell into the ground, howling: - You got me with your Linda! She will be alive!- echoed throughout the castle.

And as soon as the stone floor closed, the shoemaker wept with happiness, realizing that his dear Linda was alive. The girl opened her eyes and through a muddy thought tried to understand where she was and what had happened:

-Was it all a bad dream? Oh how long I slept. Are you with me alive? -She stroked Arthur's head with her hand.

He kissed her hand.

- Darling, it was not a dream.

- What was it then?

- It was a reality: exactly, you were dying. I thought that I would lose you. You were one step away from death.

- Ah, me?! I don't remember anything.

-The evil sorcerer scratched you hard when he was in werewolf form.

- Oh, yes, my whole body aches.

The hunchback examined her wounds - everything healed, as if nothing had happened.

Linda hugged him and felt the hump behind him.

-        What is it? Have you been bewitched?

- Yes, I was enchanted before, and now I have become myself.

He got up from the floor and covered his face with his hands.

Tears poured from his eyes down his cheeks - the guy wept bitterly, believing that he had already lost his beloved forever.

- Here I am, ugly from birth, ugly. I don't think you need me now.

-        What are you talking about? - Linda jumped up, staggering, and tried to approach the Hunchback, but he pushed her away with an outstretched hand.

-        I'm leaving. Father is waiting for me, - and turned to leave.

- Where are you going? -She grabbed his sleeve. - Do you think I'll leave you like this?

The shoemaker stopped.

-        How? What, I thought you already left me...

- Oh, you fool. How can I leave you? I really do love you.

- Look at me. Is it possible to love this? - he threw up his hands.

- And with such big beautiful and loving eyes, who else will look at me so affectionately? You have a pure soul - no one else has one. And I fell in love with you not because of gold, and not because of beauty, but because you took care of me and were betrayed.

The hunchback still did not believe. When he was handsome and fell in love with the seller of sweets, she brightened up his life, and now it is simply impossible that he could brighten up her life. And he turned back to the exit to leave, but the girl clung even tighter to his arm.

-        No, do not go! Stay with me. I fell in love with you for your tender eyes and sympathetic heart.

- But I'm ugly. Don't you notice it? People will laugh at you.

- But I don't see it. And I don't care what others say.

The hunchback wiped away his tears and remained. Hesitantly looked into her eyes and quietly, almost in a whisper, asked:

- Do you really think so? I don't believe my ears.

- Then trust your eyes. Look at me. Before you is me, Linda, your beloved.

- Beloved, - he hugged her. -So you will marry me?

- Of course, yes, otherwise why am I with you then?

And he wept for joy, clutching the most secret to his heart. Leaving the empty black castle, they drove to his father.

An old shoemaker was sitting at his house sewing up someone's old boots. Arthur left Linda to wait outside the door to prepare his father for the meeting, while he went inside. The old man was sitting in the semi-darkness when his son appeared on the threshold.

- Oh, son! He rubbed his clouded eyes. Is this not imagining me? Did you really come?

- Yes, dad. I'm real!

And they rushed to hug. Long time no see. The old man's eyes bulged.

- Don't cry, father. Now we'll never be apart again. I'm back to you for good. And even if we leave here, we already have a palace and we will all move there together.

- What palace, son, what are you talking about?

-         True true. Ten-chambered palace. I built it myself. With a wide moat, powerful carved gates, high ceilings, large windows and a young garden around.

- Did you build it? Where did you get so much money from? You and I have always barely had enough for food.

- I'll tell you about it later. We will all live there.

- Who is everyone? -said the old shoemaker.

- I hope you don't mind meeting my fiancee now?

- Bride? Do you have a bride? Are you kidding, son?

And the old man thought:

- What kind of bride does he have there, if she covets such a huge hump? Probably lame or pockmarked, or maybe even a curve-blind one. No one took her in marriage, so she agreed with grief to go for my hunchback.

He added aloud:

- Come on, bring me here, son, my beloved daughter-in-law. I agree in advance. Not one of you to while away a century.

And he imagined himself in the palace, and next to him was a lame and crooked, also hunchbacked daughter-in-law in a crumpled apron.

Arthur hurried to open the door and called Linda:

- Come in.

The girl timidly entered, looking around in embarrassment.

- What a bright and spacious room you have. How cozy it is here!

And the old shoemaker, as soon as he saw the guest, shook his finger in the air:

-         Oh-oh! Is she alive

- Dad, calm down, what are you talking about?

- Son, everyone is laughing at me. Nobody believes. One werewolf, foaming at the mouth, brought it and threw it on my bed, and another werewolf, with red eyes, rushed over and dragged it away. I told people, but they take me for a fool. And that first werewolf broke into me late at night with your fiancee and said:

- Hold, dad, your daughter-in-law. Take care of her, - and sped off.

- Hold, dad, your daughter-in-law. Take care of her, - and sped away.

- He called me his dad. And then half an hour later the second came running, even worse than before. Claws tearing and throwing. He grinds his teeth. Without a word, he grabbed her and sped away. I'm quite old age clink glasses apparently.

- What are you, dad, no, of course not. It's just that there were a lot of rumors about werewolves, that's why you fancied it, - he felt sorry for his father and did not tell him about what he had experienced and how he himself was one of those two terrible monsters.

Linda just opened her mouth to add something to this story, but Arthur, unnoticed by his father, put his finger to his lips, urging her not to talk about what had happened. The girl agreed and remained silent.

- Werewolves yes ... and her? I definitely saw her.

- Don't fill your head with nonsense, dad. Now we are all together and happy.

- Oh, - the father giggled, and whispered: - I didn't imagine her so beautiful.

And again he thought:- She must be some kind of fool, albeit a beauty. Why else would she have come to marry my poor cripple?

He continued aloud:

- Only you do not give birth to many children, otherwise they will suddenly be fools. Although I will teach fools to darn shoes. We'll live somehow.

The bride and groom looked at each other, not understanding what fools the old man was talking about. And the joyful old man ran to notify the neighbors about the upcoming wedding of his son.

And then came the long-awaited day of the wedding. Sunday afternoon, sunny morning. People dressed up, with smiles, went straight to the temple. They called not only the inhabitants of their village, but also the surrounding villages. All comers. The old shoemaker rejoiced most of all, because he did not even hope that his hunchback would ever marry, and even to such a beauty. It was like winning the lottery.

 For Linda, an airy dress with other valuable patterns was specially sewn, and she walked in it like a fairy soared through the air, and a long veil flew in the wind, creating the illusion of heaven descending to earth. And the girl shone with happiness like the rays of the sun themselves.

Arthur was also immensely happy, but doubts gnawed at him: how could she live with him, with such a hunchback. And the thought did not leave him that she was marrying him only out of pity and gratitude for everything he had done for her.

And all the villagers around were whispering, lost in conjectures who this bride was.

-She must be uglier than the groom herself,- some suggested, not yet seeing the girl.

Others argued:

- Because of the money, you will choose the devil. And this Hunchback got a little gold.

- Probably she is not one of the beauties, some kind of ugly or blind, who was deceived.

- He-he, or a beggar woman from the porch, - echoed behind. - Found a place to hang out.

And then the bells were heard on the road. The people parted to let six bay horses harnessed to a gilded carriage.

As soon as the carriage rolled up to the gate, the surprised crowd surrounded it, whispering:

Has the king himself come?

They bowed low, waiting for the sovereign himself to leave, because only he had such a beautiful cart, but a thin white handle with a handkerchief appeared from there, which the footman immediately picked up and helped the passenger to get off the ground.

-Oh, the princess must have come to congratulate our Arthur,- the people whispered.

-He probably sewed special slippers for her, so she came to thank him,- they continued to put forward various versions.

When the carriage door swung open, the crowd parted, gasping in amazement - some of them opened their mouths, and there was nothing for evil tongues to say.

From afar, only muffled sighs could be heard. And when they saw a slender leg in patent white boots, they looked up: a girl of amazing beauty stood in front of them. And the footman announced:

- The bride has arrived, make way, let her pass!

And the crowd roared, growing from a whisper into a rumble:

-        How so? Is this his fiancee?

Some handsome men patted their chests:

- This beauty should have belonged to me! What an injustice!

- I was supposed to be in the place of the groom! - the guys almost fought among themselves, which of them was more worthy of her.

Barely separated them. And it became a shame for them to go inside to look at the wedding of a freak with a beauty.

Arthur was waiting at the altar. The old shoemaker proudly led the beautiful bride, for everyone to see. And the crowd rushed after them, the children tried to grab a transparent train, make a wish for themselves. Ahead, the road was strewn with rose petals, and the vaults of the church were decorated with white lilies, a symbol of innocence.

Even the priest was dumbfounded: he had seen many miracles in his lifetime, but he had never seen such a strange couple. He wondered if it was a trick?

- We must ask the beauty, what if she is forcibly led?

Linda, flushed with excitement, all the more did not dare, out of embarrassment, to raise her eyes to the indignant crowd. Such a contrast was too embarrassing for everyone. Even little aware of what was happening children were embarrassed. They said:

- He's not a match for her.

Arthur heard these exclamations and sank even more from chagrin:

-        I made a mistake. How can I ruin her life? Lord, I made a mistake, forgive me, I'll fix everything now: I'll refuse before it's too late. I can't ruin her life for my own selfishness. For the sake of sincere love, I will give it up.

- Forgive me, my love. I don't have the strength to watch how evil tongues will condemn you all your life for crippling your fate next to me. She, I know, will find the best guy, to match herself, a slender, handsome, loving husband and will be happy with him.

And a large tear rolled down his pale cheek.

And as soon as Arthur got ready, looking directly at Linda, then at the priest with a longing look, to answer no, when suddenly the priest, breaking the tradition, unexpectedly first asked the bride if she was ready to take Arthur as her husband and spend her whole life with him in grief and in joy.

The humpbacked man opened his mouth, about to force the girl to say no, when a piercing silence hung up to the very vaults, and amid this barely breathing silence her thin, gentle voice was heard, confidently stretching out an echo:

-Yes, sir, I agree.

And suddenly it became much brighter in the church, as if everything dirty and envious was gone in an instant. The rays of the sun penetrated through the colorful stained-glass windows and illuminated all those present, as if in an instant their souls were cleansed, as if everything gloomy and vile crawled out in a black fog and with a howl, a menacing howl flew out of the doors, evaporating in the sky and rushing like a whirlwind into the black castle of the sorcerer. All at once it became easy and pleasant, the faces lit up with a childish sincere smile. At the same moment, somewhere in the distance, there was a powerful roar, like thousands of cannon shots. And clouds of gray dust flew up to the church. It's the old damned castle that has collapsed. And at the same time, a huge pillar of light descended, blinding everyone present. People blinked. And, opening their eyes, they saw that instead of a humpbacked shoemaker, there was a tall, stately, handsome young man.

-        Favorite! Linda exclaimed. - You became again the same as before, when we first met.

- God, it's a miracle! -exclaimed the priest. - Let's pray to God! May miracles happen in everyone's life. Let's thank the Almighty for a good life for all of us and for this happy couple, who today proved to us the power of true love.

A whisper of thanksgiving ran through all directions.

The satisfied priest asked the groom:

- And you, Arthur, do you agree to marry Linda and become her support and caring, loving husband?

- Yes, of course yes! How could it be otherwise?! -exclaimed the happy groom.

-Our love has always been selfless,- the happy bride smiled.

And the crowd proclaimed:

- Praise God!

He brought his father to his castle and, having played a magnificent wedding, they lived happily. Nobody envied them anymore. Everyone rejoiced at their happiness. And on such a significant day, Arthur presented all the guests with gold. And they lived happily ever after. Arthur opened his shoe factory, hired his fellow villagers, teaching them his craft. And in all cities and villages they only had time to make orders, increasing the demand for his comfortable and fashionable shoes.